A RUSSIAN FAREWELL

Also written and illustrated by Leonard Everett Fisher

Picture Books
PUMPERS, BOILERS, HOOKS AND LADDERS
PUSHERS, SPADS, JENNIES AND JETS
A HEAD FULL OF HATS

Nonfiction
THE COLONIAL AMERICANS (19 Volumes)
  Glassmakers, Silversmiths, Printers, Papermakers, Wigmakers, Hatters, Shoe-
  makers, Tanners, Potters, Limners, Shipbuilders, Homemakers, Cabinetmakers,
  Architects, Weavers, Peddlers, Schoolmasters, Doctors, Blacksmiths
TWO IF BY SEA
PICTURE BOOK OF REVOLUTIONARY WAR HEROES
THE ART EXPERIENCE: OIL PAINTING 15–19th CENTURY
THE LIBERTY BOOK
ALPHABET ART
NINETEENTH CENTURY AMERICA (Series in Preparation)
  Railroads, Factories, Hospitals

Fiction
THE DEATH OF EVENING STAR
THE WARLOCK OF WESTFALL
SWEENEY'S GHOST
ACROSS THE SEA FROM GALWAY
LETTERS FROM ITALY
NOONAN
THE JETTY

A RUSSIAN FÆREWELL

WRITTEN AND ILLUSTRATED BY
LEONARD EVERETT FISHER

FOUR WINDS PRESS ☙ NEW YORK

LIBRARY OF CONGRESS CATALOGING IN PUBLICATION DATA

Fisher, Leonard Everett.
A Russian farewell.

Summary: Depicts the anti-Semitic terror that finally drives
Benjamin Shapiro, his wife, and 11 children out of Czarist
Russia to America at the beginning of the 20th century.
[1. Jews in Russia—Fiction. 2. Russia—History—
1904–1914—Fiction] I. Title
PZ7.F533Ru   [Fic]   80-342   ISBN 0-590-07525-X

PUBLISHED BY FOUR WINDS PRESS

A DIVISION OF SCHOLASTIC MAGAZINES, INC.,

NEW YORK, N.Y.

PRINTED IN THE UNITED STATES OF AMERICA

LIBRARY OF CONGRESS CATALOG CARD NUMBER: 80-342

1 2 3 4 5 84 83 82 81 80

◙ FOREWORD ◙

A Russian Farewell by Leonard Everett Fisher is a historical novel based on a family saga as it was lived, with the persons, history, and events drawn from actuality. Nevertheless, in the interest of fiction, some characters and occurrences have either been invented or altered. The introduction of these inventions, alterations, and characterizations does not in any way disturb the flow of history or the destinies of those whose experiences are herein related.

It is the third book of a trilogy for young readers by Mr. Fisher dealing with Irish, Italian, and Jewish emigration to the United States between 1849 and 1906. The first book, *Across the Sea from Galway*, involves the Irish famine of the mid-nineteenth century. The second, *Letters from Italy*, deals with the lack of economic opportunity in Italy at the end of the nineteenth century. This third volume, *A Russian Farewell*, centers on the terror that drove the Jews out of Czarist Russia at the beginning of the twentieth century.

A RUSSIAN FÆREWELL

PROLOGUE

✺ **1904 - 1906** ✺

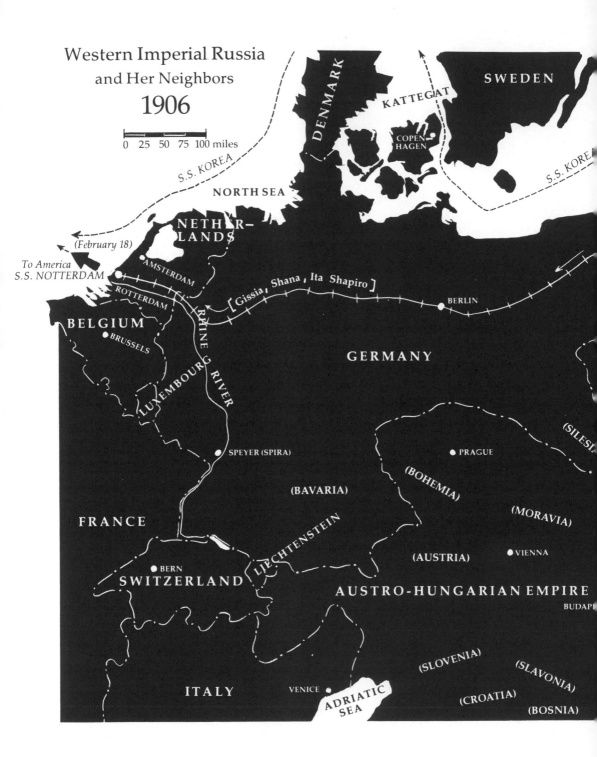

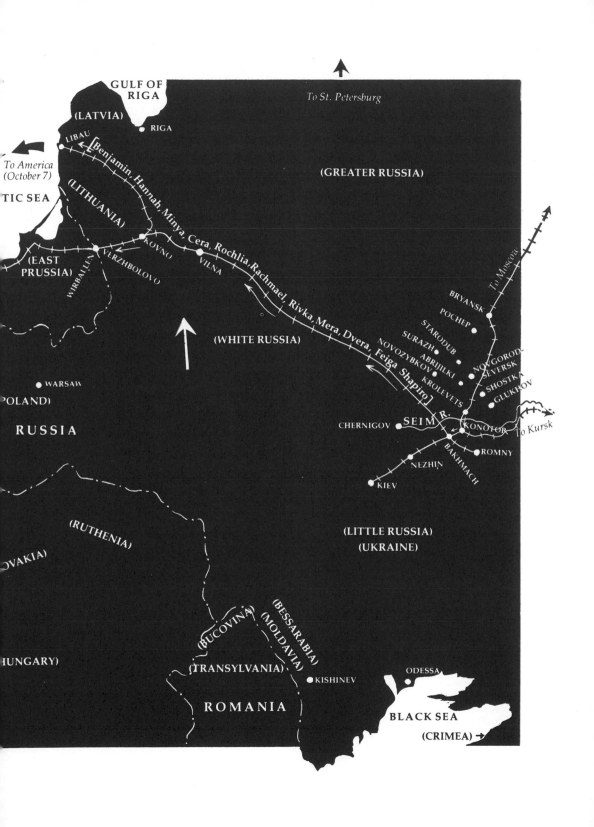

Unlike Julius Caesar's Gaul that was divided into three parts, the Russian Empire of Nicholas II, whose twenty-three-year reign included the years 1904 through 1906, was divided into four parts.

Foremost was *Greater Russia,* the northern sector of the country west of the Ural Mountains. It was the most westernized part of European Russia and included the great cities of St. Petersburg and Moscow.

Next and eastward beyond the Ural Mountains that divided Europe from Asia was *Siberian Russia.* Here was a vast dreary landscape set in an interminable emptiness that finally slid into the roaring surf of the Pacific Ocean. The whole of this immense wilderness, peopled by convicts, exiles, and Asiatic nomads, was crossed by the unfinished Trans-Siberian Railroad. The line's 4,350 miles of track joined Mother Russia to her aims and possessions in the Far East.

Understandably, the Japanese viewed the coming of a Russian railroad with suspicion and alarm. The Russian presence in Manchuria, in North Korea, and in the powerful naval base at Port Arthur on the Yellow Sea had already unsettled them. The Japanese, having beaten China in a war in 1895, now had plans of their own for the Asian mainland, and none of these included the Russians. On February 8, 1904, Japan attacked Port Arthur without warning and quickly immobilized the Russian fleet. Over the next year, the Russians were continually beaten wherever they fought. Surprised and shocked, the world watched as the unheralded Japanese became the "yellow peril" and strutted to victory in 1905 with recognition as a world power.

Below Siberian Russia, to the south and west, was *Asiatic*

Russia, a rugged land of time-worn civilizations. The area pressed the western fringe of China and skirted the rim of northern Iran and other parts of the Near East.

Lastly was *Little Russia* in the southwest — eighty thousand square miles that included the Ukraine, Russia's "breadbasket." Here, in this congested acreage known since 1762 as the "Pale of Settlement," was the territory Empress Catherine the Great of Russia had set aside for thousands of Jews she did not care to have near her. Five million Jews lived in collective fear of ten million frustrated, illiterate non-Jewish peasants whose hold on life was often more flimsy than that of their Jewish neighbors. The fear was very real.

By April of 1903 the Jews thought that the worst had passed. During the early 1880s, blood-letting pogroms against Jews had been so terrible that many fled to America. Since that time there had been a mood of civility and hope. But the dream was shattered in Kishinev, the sophisticated capital city of Russian Moldavia on the Romanian border. In two mind-numbing days of April 1903, the Jews of Russia knew the extent of the madness of which the human soul was capable.

Fifty thousand Jews — roughly half the population of Kishinev — were dragged into the streets and brutally assaulted. Death and ruin were everywhere within the Jewish community. Men, women, children, and infants were beaten, robbed, raped, mangled, and killed. Heads of state around the world protested the barbarism.

Pope Pius X publicly condemned the savage mutilation and offered what help he could to the Jewish survivors of Kishinev. The Jews of Russia held the Czar's Minister of the Interior, Vyacheslav Konstantinovich Plehve, responsible for the massacre. Plehve's policy for calming restless peasants unhappy with their own miserable lot was publicly stated: "Drown the revolution in Jewish blood."

Jewish terrorists caught up with Plehve a year later and murdered him. From that assassination on, no Jew anywhere in Russia felt safe in bed. The situation worsened still when the Governor General of Moscow, Grand Duke Sergei, the Czar's uncle, was assassinated in February 1905, following Russia's surrender of Port Arthur to the Japanese. And those Jews who once believed they could survive with some decency and peace now had second thoughts.

From that time on, millions of Jews in southwest Russia (nearly all that there were in Russia) worked out their lives denied a full measure of life's amenities; they were prohibited from fully entering the mainstream of Russian life. Jews, including Muscovite Samuel Poliakov, chief architect of the Russian railroad system, were even banned from Moscow. There were exceptions. But in this land of no promise, where hope was sucked from a human being, it took enormous stamina, wit, and minor miracles to survive, not to mention an unshakable faith in God.

Most Jews in Little Russia, bewildered by God's lack of compassion for His own children, turned their insufferable lives inward, mystically toward God, seeking the reasons for their lot in so inhospitable a world. Many withdrew from reality and searched their Torah, Talmud, Mishna, and Gemara — their ancient histories, interpretations, and commentaries — for a clue to their deliverance. Shorn of all hope but never of their self-respect, and clinging to their historical, Biblical past, the Russian Jews, like no other Jews, succeeded in submerging

[6]

their tears and captivity in God's own Books. They could read. And because they could read they could find solace for their anguish. The more anguish, the more they read. The more they read, the more they endured the most unendurable. And when they came to the end of their readings they turned to the first page and started all over again. They would survive.

"*Sh'ma Yis-ro-ayl: A-dō-noy Elō-hay-nu, A-dō-noy e-hod.* Hear O Israel: The Lord Our God, the Lord is One."

❧ 1904 ☙

❧ ONE ❧

The small, unpainted, wooden stationhouse, gray as the bleak and lifeless autumn sky but now temporarily festooned with the white, blue, and red colors of Imperial Russia, hugged the southbound track of the new Moscow–Kiev Railroad Line. The sign over the platform door said:

KROLEVETS

A noisy, surging mass of people extended along both sides of the gleaming tracks for about two miles, spilling onto the rails at various points. The throng had been gathering since noon waiting to be touched by progress and power — by a train and Czar Nicholas II, emperor of all the Russias.

Standing quietly in the crowd opposite the stationhouse on the northbound side of the track was a lanky, bearded three-some, Benjamin Shapiro and two of his three younger brothers. Bundled against the late afternoon chill in fur hats; short, belted, woolen tunics; and heavy, loose-fitting pants tucked into dusty, knee-high, thick leather boots, the brothers Shapiro surveyed the crowd and the uniformed group on the platform. Occasionally, they would peer into the distant gloom and look for the train. Benjamin would then impatiently pull a weighty gold watch from under his tunic, look at the time, look down the track, shake the watch near his ear, look at the time again, and finally put the piece away. Gregor Suchenko, the newly appointed stationmaster, caught Benjamin's eye and gave him

[12]

a nod. Benjamin returned the casual recognition with another nod.

Benjamin Shapiro, a leading figure among Krolevets's three thousand Jews, had been invited to stand with the official party on the station platform. He declined the dubious honor of being the only Jew there, preferring to greet the train and the Czar in the company of his brothers, Tevya, a newlywed, and Hilya, a bachelor. More importantly, however, was the fact that the forty-five-year-old Benjamin, father of nine daughters and one son, was momentarily expecting his wife, Hannah, to deliver another child; he was hoping for a boy. Consequently, he did not want to be tied down to an official party.

Benjamin's third brother, David, was in America, alive and well in New York City. David never wrote to anyone. He entrusted this chore to his sister, Chana, who he knew would at least keep his memory alive in Krolevets.

Chana Shapiro Weinstein and her husband, Samuel, left Krolevets soon after their marriage and went to America. They settled in Hart Street, Brooklyn, where Samuel scratched out a living in the Wallabout Market as a wholesale dealer in fruit and produce. There, in Brooklyn, the Weinsteins kept an eye on their own growing family of first-born Americans and half an eye on David. Chana wrote to her sister-in-law regularly. Usually, she would end her letters with "David says hello," or, "David sends regards."

David had spent nearly four years in the Czar's army. He was drafted and promptly disappeared. Had it not been for Benjamin's persistence, David might have been lost forever. Benjamin, whose business as a wholesale meat dealer included the army as a customer, used a business connection, Quartermaster Major Andrei Simienko, to find David. It took the major three years to locate him. When he did, he had David transferred to a garrison near home where Benjamin was permitted to buy his brother's release.

"You were not meant to be a soldier, David, a Jewish soldier in the Czar's army," Benjamin told him. "Go. Leave this place. Jew or not, once a soldier, always a soldier. They will come after you again."

David heeded the warning. He left for America soon after. There, in New York City, he hid from every uniformed authority, including the streetcar conductor, and he rarely ventured out in daylight.

Benjamin Shapiro was the rock of his family and the anchor of Krolevets's Jews. Hannah had dominion over the family, whether Benjamin realized this or not. But Benjamin was the shield that protected them all from the hostile world they lived in. He owned a delicatessen store, in addition to his meat-provisioning business, that was popular with Jew and Gentile alike. He had inherited the store upon the death of his father, Rachmael, thirty-four years before, in 1870. Benjamin was only eleven years old at the time. His grieving mother had no choice but to put the boy in charge. Once in a while Uncle Ara, his father's brother, would look in on him to see how he was getting along. Young Benjamin needed no help. He knew how to win friends and survive. He made sure that the poor, Jew or Gentile, would not starve. And before he was twenty, he was managing the affairs of his synagogue, Beth Israel.

But more important than the delicatessen, with its tantalizing odors of sour pickles and corned meats, was the license he possessed authorizing him to sell meat to the Russian army. The

[15]

certificate was from a government agency, the *Gildiya Kupyet*, which officially permitted him, in the name of the Czar, to deal with the army. It was a rare opportunity for a Jew in Czarist Russia.

Benjamin had inherited the authorization, like the delicatessen, from his father. He had become the head of the family when Rachmael died. Tevya, Hilya, and David inherited nothing. They simply worked for Benjamin. Their sisters, Chana and Etarivka, also inherited nothing. They had to marry young to survive with some security. Unlike Chana who fled to America with her husband, Etarivka married Louis Bunisch and moved to Bakhmach, a sizable town about thirty-five miles southwest of Krolevets.

Rachmael Shapiro, their father, had inherited the original license from *his* father who received the *Gildiya Kupyet* certificate as a reward for feeding Russian troops bivouacked in and around Krolevets during the Crimean War of the 1850s. Benjamin made good use of the certificate when Russia fought the Turks in 1877, and once again there were troops nearby. Since that early time, Benjamin, his brothers, and various uncles and cousins elsewhere sold meat to the army garrisons scattered throughout their region (chiefly field units of the Ninth and Twenty-first Army Corps headquartered in Kiev, the capital of Little Russia), the Ukraine. The family's long connection with the military establishment gave them a slight edge in the explosive Ukraine. No violence was directed against them during the bloody pogroms of the 1880s, nor against any other Jew in Krolevets, although murderous episodes took place all around them and on occasion still did.

Now that Russia was embroiled in yet another war, this time in the Far East with Japan, business boomed. Benjamin's

[16]

authorization relieved him of a variety of restrictions that hampered the activities of most Jews. While no Jew could travel beyond a limited distance away from his town — his shtetl — without a police permit, Benjamin could use his certificate to travel anywhere in Russia on army business without prior police approval. He was free to come and go as he pleased. Still, he was only slightly less of an outcast than his fellow Jews. He was part of a system. He reasoned that as long as the system needed him, so long as he could provide a necessary service and obey the rules, things would work out.

His reputation among non-Jews was excellent. His business dealings were correct, fair, and honest. He received grudging respect from Krolevets's Gentiles for contributing to the Czar's Fund for War Widows and Orphans; for sending platters of corned beef and sour pickles to the beggars huddled around fires in Alexander I Square; and for quietly donating a few kopeks regularly to Gregor Suchenko for the Candle Fund of Krolevets's Church of Our Saviour on the east side of the square.

"Here, Suchenko, my old friend, take this. Buy some candles for your church. May the Lord bless you and keep you."

Benjamin never knew what Suchenko did with the money. It mattered little. Although they had known each other since boyhood, they were hardly close friends. Suchenko was an opportunist who seemed to be in many places at the same time. He was a friendly and harmless soul; however, Benjamin never knew how far Suchenko could be trusted.

Benjamin Shapiro liked his town as it was and his life in it. His family had lived in the place since 1794 when Jews were permitted to settle there. It was a town where three thousand Jews somehow or other got along with nine thousand Chris-

[17]

tians. Krolevets was a quiet town. And no one dared ask why, although they appreciated Benjamin's line of business communication with the Christian world and understood how less vulnerable they all were because of it. Still, no one spoke about it. No one wished to spark the explosion of trouble they knew was just over the next hill and long overdue, or brewing every day in the noisy mix of the marketplace on Alexander I Square.

The square was the hub of Krolevets's energies. Surrounded by stone, wood, and stucco buildings shielded by chestnut trees, the square was breached at its four corners by four unpaved roads. Here was Shapiro's Delicatessen. Next door were Berkhan and Morozovski, the photographers. Next door to them was a horse trader. On the other side of the delicatessen was Bronstein, the tailor. There were a bakery, cloth merchant, and variety shop that sold pots, pans, combs, and buttons. There were fruit and produce stalls and a kosher butcher supplied by the Shapiros. Opposite the Church of Our Saviour, on the west side of the square, stood Beth Israel, Krolevets's Jewish synagogue, a plain, gray, two-story building.

Krolevets was not paradise. But in the Imperial Russia of 1904, as far as Benjamin Shapiro was concerned, it would do.

Yet, he did have some doubts that nagged him from time to time. Often he wondered whether or not the rules would ever change to include all of his children. How distressing it had been to decide which one of his children should receive a sound practical education in a Russian school. The law allowed only one "qualified" child from a Jewish family to enroll. All other secular education was illegal. The Russian Gentiles could send to school as many children as they had.

That was six years ago when Hannah and Benjamin had only seven children: Gissia, thirteen; Minya, twelve; Shana, eleven;

Cera, ten; Ita, nine; Rochlia, eight; and Rachmael, three. Rivka, Mera, Feiga, and Dvera were yet unborn.

Hannah and Benjamin decided that instead of one of the younger girls being enrolled in the elementary school, one of the older girls should try for acceptance in the Gymnasium — the high school. It was a gamble. An entrance examination was required. But if they were successful, whoever was chosen would quickly become a teacher to the rest.

Minya was thought to be the only one clever enough to pass the difficult examination. Besides, at twelve, she seemed to be the right age. Minya took the test and passed. She was admitted and graduated four years later (two years ago) in 1902. From the very beginning of Minya's formal education, she began giving lessons to her sisters. Gissia, Shana, Cera, Ita, and Rochlia had no difficulty absorbing Minya's education. Minya graduated with honors. The possibility of going on to the university in Kiev was alive in her mind. She could live with Uncle Herschel Borodin, Hannah's brother, a physician who had graduated the medical school there. But this would have to be put off for a few years. Minya became a teacher, secretly, to the Jewish children of Krolevets. She taught them reading, writing, arithmetic, geography, and everything that she had learned at the Gymnasium. These subjects could not have been learned in the hadarim — in the religious Hebrew schools.

There was an order to things in Krolevets, a pattern, a rhythm of life in which everyone had a part. It was fixed as it had been forever, so long as the rules remained the same and everyone obeyed the rules, more or less. But now the sleepy, orderly town was about to be awakened from its long nap by the toot of a train whistle.

[19]

⚅ TWO ⚅

Less than a month ago the railroad tracks now piercing Krolevets were nowhere to be seen. Only an endless, timeless,
wagon-rutted dirt road disappeared into some woods and
wandered south about twenty-five miles to Konotop, where
Uncle Ara Shapiro and his brood lived. Only the Seim River interrupted the road and its ruts. Konotop, once an impregnable
fortress town on the old Russo–Polish frontier, was already a
station stop on the important east-west Kursk–Kiev Railroad
completed earlier in the year.

The old road meandered a few miles past the Konotop peat
marshes south to Bakhmach, where it ran into the Romny–
Libau Railroad. Bakhmach had become an important rail stop in
recent years as the north-south Romny–Libau line became Russia's principal railroad in the west. The line linked the fertile,
densely Jewish Ukraine in the south with ports on the Baltic
Sea more than six hundred miles to the north. Libau, a Latvian
city and port terminus of the line, would become an escape
hatch out of Little Russia for many a Jew after the turn of the
century. Bakhmach would become the junction, the transfer
point, from Krolevets to Libau.

The Romny–Libau Railroad began its service in 1881, the
same year assassins blew up Czar Alexander II on a St.
Petersburg bridge. His successor, Alexander III, took the opportunity to unleash pogroms, unspeakable horrors of death
and destruction, upon the blameless Jews who had all they
could do just to stay alive. For centuries in Europe it had been a

customary pastime in days of national stress and uncertainty to let unfortunate peasants kill unhappy Jews. And this they did in Russia for three years — following the murder of Alexander II — usually during the Easter season. Five Christian assassins were hanged for the murder. And hundreds of Jews were killed for their innocence. So intense was the reign of terror, conducted with savage certainty against the Jews in full view of the world, that thousands sought safety in America and elsewhere. By the beginning of World War I in 1914, a generation after the assassination of Alexander II, two million of Russia's five million Jews would be driven to America.

Once out of Bakhmach, the well-rutted road swung northwest through seventy miles of picturesque orchards to Chernigov, the one-thousand-year-old capital city of the "black earth" district, also called Chernigov.

Ten days ago, the last section of track along the 530-mile stretch connecting Moscow with the once proud capital city of all the Russias, Kiev, was spiked into place at Bryansk, the near-halfway point. Only a week ago, the last nail was hammered into the sign of the undistinguished Krolevets station. Yesterday, Saturday, as Krolevets's Jews prayed in their synagogue, the station bell was bolted to a post on the station platform — the final touch.

The stationhouse was a recent addition to the near-leafless landscape that surrounded it just north of town. Two weeks ago, no building stood where this one now stands. The nearest structure had been a half mile down the track — a broken-down, thatched-roof shack on the edge of Krolevets — the edge of the world as far as its former Jewish occupants were concerned.

[21]

❧ THREE ❧

Now it was Sunday, October 16, 1904 — October 29, 1904 everyplace else in the world. Russia, faithful to the ancient calendar devised by Julius Caesar's Romans, was thirteen days behind everyone else. The first train to clatter through the rural quiet of Krolevets was expected to stop at the station shortly — at 5 p.m., to be exact.

The train had left Moscow's Bryansk Station on schedule at one minute past midnight. It was due to arrive in Kiev twenty-one hours later at 9 p.m., after additional stops at Konotop, Bakhmach, and Nezhin. Rumor had it that this was to be a ceremonial running of the train to inaugurate the new line. The word had been passed up and down the line that Czar Nicholas II would be aboard the train ready to greet his subjects all along the route.

"That's the most ridiculous thing I've heard in weeks," Benjamin Shapiro told his pregnant wife, Hannah, as he prepared to go out to the tracks to see for himself. "Imagine!" he mused, "the Czar getting on a train so late at night! I shall never forget how I froze on the night train from Bakhmach to Romny. When was that? Two years ago? Three? What's the difference. If I were the Czar, I would be in bed at that hour or take an earlier train."

"Is there an earlier train, Benjamin?" Hannah asked her husband, feigning ignorance in such worldly matters.

"No. Not today."

"So?"

"So that is why I would be home in bed," Benjamin replied

[22]

with mock arrogance and a slight twinkle as he bowed and left for the station.

There at the station, Gregor Suchenko, the newly appointed stationmaster (he was also the newly appointed ticket agent, baggage transfer agent, and information clerk in addition to being the Krolevets postmaster, town telegrapher, and tobacconist), was at the platform bell ready to do his duty and ring in the train. Until now, Suchenko had done all of his official business from his tobacco shop directly across Alexander I Square from Shapiro's Delicatessen. Although the post office itself was next door to the church, no one bought their postage stamps there, nor had their packages inspected, weighed, and registered there, nor paid whatever fees and taxes the Post Office Department required. All this was done in Suchenko's shop. The only thing anyone went to the post office for was to pick up mail or deliver mail for transmission — mail that had been prepaid to Suchenko.

Suchenko could also send and receive telegraphic messages in a back room of the shop. Soon, however, his equipment would be dismantled and rebuilt at the railroad station where he would have to schedule some of his time for handling railroad affairs and operating the telegraph. He was fully prepared, nevertheless, to sell train and baggage tickets over the counter in his tobacco shop. The situation plainly called for some hired help.

Behind Suchenko, poised at the bell, stood Chief of Police Tartazov; members of the Krolevets Town Council; members of the Krolevets Town Board; and the fiercely mustachioed mayor of Krolevets, Boris Alexeyevitch Grozni, reputed to be a direct descendant of that most feared of all Russian rulers, Ivan

[23]

Grozni — Ivan the Terrible. Actually, there was no truth to the mayor's descendancy. He was a round, pompous bureaucrat with no sense of humor, who encouraged everyone to believe his awesome ancestry. No one did.

The entire official party was resplendent in blue uniforms trimmed with brass buttons and gold epaulets. Mayor Grozni stood out from the rest by wearing the white, blue, and red sash of his office across his ample torso. Chief of Police Tartazov wore a menacing curved sword that dangled from his leather belt and dragged along the ground behind him.

A lookout was posted high in the bright blue onion-shaped belfry of the Church of Our Saviour back in the center of town. The bellringer, grisly old Feodor Korbeyev, stood attentively at his rope, ready to herald the arrival of the train and its distinguished passenger with a great clanging and banging of the church bells.

The Jews of Krolevets learned a great deal from Feodor Korbeyev and his bells. Every important occasion was ceremoniously prefaced by a ringing of the bells. Each edict and decree issued by the Czar; each new law, regulation, and statute; every wedding, birth, baptism, confirmation, death, and excommunication; and every holiday on the religious calendar was signaled by Feodor Korbeyev and his bells. Krolevets did not have a newspaper or a print shop of its own to do the work.

The Jews paid strict attention to the music of the bells. Sometimes it was meant for them alone. Every official humiliation designed to humble them since their arrival in Krolevets a little more than a hundred years ago — additional taxes and tribute; travel restrictions; punishments for alleged crimes against the Czar; cancellation of education privileges; voiding of property

[24]

ownership; reinstatements of voided deeds; curfews and what-not — was tolled by an extra chorus of the bells. Now the bells would teach them about trains.

"Must it always be like this?" Rabbi Itzak Sarchefsky cried out one day.

"Yes, Rabbi, so it must be, always," replied Yuri Malinikov, a schoolteacher. "You Jews are wretched and narrow. You are to be pitied that you are not like us. You live too much in the past, not enough in the present, and not at all in the future. One day you shall all see the truth and the light."

The rabbi did not like what he had heard. Violence was but a subtle threat in Krolevets — a constant intimidation festering beneath the surface. Lately, however, more Jewish windows seemed to be broken; more old Jews were "accidentally" tripped up on the square and sent sprawling, and there seemed to be more obscenities hurled at Jews than before. No one considered these to be particularly worrisome. These were small "annoyances" when compared to what Europe's Jews had had to endure for time beyond recall. Besides, Jews were used to these things, the rabbi told himself. He tried to let it pass, but the schoolteacher Malinikov's reply was not meant to be a piece of intellectual dialogue. The reply would not go away — "One day you shall all see the truth and the light." This time it was a threat, a prediction of things to come.

"And why not?" the rabbi mumbled to himself. "Why should we expect anything to be different for us? It is too unrealistic."

Sunday worshippers by now had come and gone, celebrating mass, taking communion, giving confessions, and lighting candles for the health of the Czar, the Czarina, and the rest of the royal family, and for the safety of the sons of Mother Russia

[26]

who for the past nine months had been battling the Japanese in the Far East.

Beth Israel Synagogue had no belfry. There were no lookouts posted either. It stood empty, quietly aloof from the unfolding drama, mindful of its own history and age. It was noisy enough yesterday and the night before, Friday night, as the congregants prayed for deliverance and salvation; they recounted a time-worn tale of their origins and blessed the Czar's warriors, wishing them all eternal glory, but not too quick a victory. Every Jew there knew that as long as the Czar and his ministers were preoccupied terrorizing a foreign power, they would be too busy to terrorize them.

"Long live the Czar!" shouted Rabbi Sarchefsky.

"Long live the Czarina!" shouted the congregation in one clear voice that startled the rabbi. He was more used to the discordant babble of several hundred voices, all pleading to God for help but never in unison.

"To victory!" concluded the rabbi. "But please, God, not too soon," he softly purred under his beard, not wanting to be overheard by any of the Czar's secret agents who were known to frequent the synagogue on Friday nights looking for signs of treason and perhaps a prospective soldier or two.

No one suspected that the situation in the Far East was on the brink of a Russian disaster. It was not the Czar's vaunted soldiers who were terrorizing the Japanese. It was the Japanese terrorizing the troops of Imperial Russia. The Japanese were systematically subduing the Czar's army and navy in the Far East.

The Jews returned to their prayer books and worried whether or not God was listening to them.

[27]

✪ FOUR ✪

"Gissia," Hannah called out. "Gissia? Are you there?"

"No, Mrs. Shapiro, only me," answered Dinah. The recent bride of Judah Labe, Benjamin's wagonmaster and jack-of-all-trades, poked her head into the tiny overheated room where Hannah Borodin Shapiro was waiting to bring another child into the Jewish world of Russian Krolevets.

The last thing Hannah needed was another girl around the house. She already had a small army of daughters. But when Judah Labe brought his teenage bride to live in the Shapiro barn with him, temporarily until they could find a place of their own (Judah's only home these past few years had been the barn), Dinah almost immediately became one of the family. She attached herself to Hannah and the children, and they in turn adopted her with affection.

"But don't get too close to them," Judah warned his new wife. "You are not a Shapiro. You are a Labe. Someday we shall leave them behind. I have ideas. America. Palestine. Who knows? We are not going to stay here forever. They are nice people. They have been very good to me. And I would do anything for them. But don't get too close. The parting will be too difficult for all of us."

Despite her husband's advice, Dinah became another "daughter," another "sister." Abandoned as an infant and never having had a family of her own, she could hardly help herself. For their part, the Shapiros, especially Hannah, were captivated by Dinah's warmth and well-meaning.

"Is it time, Mrs. Shapiro? You promised. . . ."

Hannah, propped up on a hill of pillows, put aside the letter she had been reading and looked down at her stomach.

"No. Nothing yet, Dinah."

"Are you sure, Mrs. Shapiro?"

"Of course I am sure, you simple girl. Don't you think I know by now?" Hannah replied with amused impatience, as the nineteen-year procession of births flashed through her mind: Gissia, now nineteen, still unmarried, Hannah's chief deputy for running the household; Minya, their eighteen-year-old school-teaching scholar; Shana, seventeen, a gifted seamstress who made and repaired most of their clothing; Cera, at sixteen, the family and business bookkeeper; Ita, fifteen, Gissia's assistant in charge of the younger children — Rochlia, twelve; Rachmael, seven; Rivka, six; Mera, four; and Feiga, two, a deaf-mute.

"I promise to let you know the minute I feel the baby is ready. In the meantime, please fetch Gissia — Minya and Shana too," she added. "Where are they?"

"They are in the back room, I think. I'll go see."

Hannah Borodin was left an orphan in Kiev and brought up by an aunt and uncle in Romny, a town about sixty miles south of Krolevets in the district of Sumy. Romny was not that much larger than Krolevets. The town's importance to the economy of western Russia, however, was quickly established when, in 1881, it became the southern end of the newly completed Romny–Libau Railroad. Within weeks of the line's completion, the rivalry between Jewish and Christian commercial interests became so bitter that the assassination of Czar Alexander II was used as an excuse for the non-Jewish merchants to support violent anti-Jewish pogroms to rid themselves of their competitors — the Jews. Somehow or other, the Borodins of Romny emerged safe and sound.

When Hannah married Benjamin in 1883 during the turmoil, as a bride of nineteen, she brought to the comfortable rural Shapiros a sophistication they hardly expected. Benjamin's mother, Dvera, thirteen years a widow, was altogether too suspicious at first of this pretty, perky girl who "stole" her eldest son away from her. But soon she succumbed to Hannah's charm, dignity, and wit, especially after Hannah personally insisted that Dvera live with them.

Although reared in a small town away from the big city of her birth, Hannah was no country bumpkin. She came from a family of durable intellectuals who belonged to that uncommon upper middle class of Russian Jews — the burgess. Her secular education — reading, writing, and numbers — was left to tutors. Her religious education was personally supervised by Romny's formidable Rabbi, Eliezer Arlosoroff.

Hannah's older brother, Herschel, a practicing physician in Kiev, was a graduate of Vladimir University Medical School. Fivel, another brother, was a printer, while still another brother, Cyril, was a student at Kiev's Polytechnic Institute. Her sister, Besha, brought up by other relatives, had completely disappeared.

Hannah was reared in a pleasant home, preoccupied only with Romny's Jewish Home for the Aged, and *Trumpeldor*, an organization for creating Jewish farm communities — kibbutzim — in Palestine.

To Hannah's lively mind, settlement in Palestine, the historic homeland of the Jews, would be a marvelous fulfillment. It would be new, fresh, free and unthreatened, a place where Jews would not be outcasts. She felt no ties to Czarist Russia, however privileged her life seemed to be. She was still a Jew in a hostile land. Her aunt and uncle had died. All that she had known in Romny was gone. She had no idea where her sister was. Her brothers managed to visit on holidays. After Feiga's birth two years ago, Herschel came more often. Feiga's deafness and muteness was a medical puzzle. Nothing could be done for her. Instead, Herschel found himself treating Benjamin for an ulcer. He prescribed goat's milk, no more smoking, and no vodka. Benjamin did as he was told and kept a goat nearby. The ulcer would subside when Benjamin remembered to do what he was told. Hannah had no obligations beyond her children and Benjamin. Hannah, at forty, was ready to leave Krolevets and start a new life.

Once she approached Benjamin with the idea of settling in Palestine. She had overheard Judah and Dinah discussing such a plan. Dinah shrank from the notion. Judah was determined to see it through one day. Benjamin was aghast.

"How can you condemn us to fry in the desert? Do you want our children to live in a tent with camels? Are you mad, Hannah? Palestine? Nonsense!" Hannah never mentioned Palestine again.

She shifted her position on the bed, staring at the letter again, and sighed. It was from her sister-in-law Chana in New York. Chana had increased her letter writing after the Kishinev massacres had stunned the world last year. She pleaded with them to get out of Russia before it was too late. Benjamin raged with each letter.

"Krolevets is not Kishinev. We are small, quiet, and civilized here. Who bothers us? We have nothing anybody wants. We are in nobody's way. We are reasonably safe here; as safe and as happy as a Jew can be anywhere," he insisted. "We have a

[31]

little more than most. I am a respected burgher. I am a Russian — Jew that I am. We Shapiros have lived here in peace for a very long time. . . ."

"One hundred and nine years only," Hannah reminded him, "a scratch on a whale's back. God created the world 5663 years ago and Krolevets was the last thing on His mind!"

"Good! You can count! Has it been so bad here?"

"How do I know? Do I look like I am 109 years old?"

"Tell me, Hannah, do you think life for a Jew is any better anywhere else in the world? No!" Benjamin declared, answering his own question.

"Yes!" replied Hannah.

"Where? Show me on a map!"

"A map! Who's got a map!"

"Minya has a map."

"I do not need a map to tell you where it is better."

"Where?"

"America! That's where."

"America! Where the streets are paved with gold, I suppose. How can you believe such stories? Enough! No more talk about how much better it is someplace else. We make do with what we are and what we have here. Here I am a very poor man among the rich. But among the poor, I am a rich man. Anyplace else I would still be a very poor man among the rich, but I would also be a very poor man among the poor. That is what would be in store for us in America, and who knows where else."

Hannah decided not to listen to Benjamin's tirades anymore. She was pregnant again. The baby was due at any moment. Benjamin's mother was dead and buried a year ago. This baby would be named for her. The Kishinev massacre could happen

[32]

again, anywhere, anytime — "now, tonight in Krolevets!" Hannah told herself. "My children! My children! What would become of them? Murdered! Raped! Tortured! For what? Why? Because my stubborn husband thinks he has a private paradise! It is insane to stay here! Benjamin must be made to understand. He has no one left to care for but us. Let Hilya and Tevya and Etarivka decide their own lives, not mine! We must do what we must do. God give me strength. Chana, we are coming!"

Hannah gazed at the letter. The child within her kicked. Hannah winced. She read the letter again.

Dear Hannah:
Why does my brother not listen? Why is he so stubborn? Is he blind? Leave Russia now! Leave before it is too late. We beg you. Samuel and I and the children are all fine. We are not millionaires in America – not yet. It is crowded where we live in Brooklyn. It is not so peaceful as I remember it in Krolevets. We struggle with our lives but we do not fear for them. We are happier here because we do not live in Benjamin's fool's paradise. Here there is a future. For you and yours there is no future. Danger and death are your handmaidens. You are not as well-off as you think. You must make Benjamin see that. I have given up trying to convince Hilya and Tevya. Etarivka doesn't even answer my letters. Are she and Louis alive? Louis thinks he knows everything. After all, he's a schoolteacher. Some teacher! I do not think he can write! Believe me, I feel sorry for the children of Bakhmach. We pray for all of you. We want to see you and the children we have never seen. Samuel will not go back. Not even to visit. So you must come here and see the nieces and nephews you have never seen. They are not Russians, you know. They are

[33]

Americans. It is time, Hannah. You must convince Benjamin.
You must make plans. You owe that much to your children and
to the unborn. God bless and keep you. David sends regards.

Yours,
Chana W.

Hannah slipped the letter under the bottom pillow. She put her hands on her stomach, feeling the unborn life within. She gazed at the empty whitewashed wall ahead and wondered where it would all end.

"Not in Krolevets," she vowed to herself.

▣ FIVE ▣

The three girls popped into the room, breathless and worried.

"Are you all right, Mama?" Gissia wanted to know.

"Yes. Yes, I am all right. I have something I want to say to you before Papa comes back from the station, and before you have a new brother or sister to care for. Where's Dinah?"

"Dinah's in the back room with the little ones," Shana said.

"Good. Dinah is one of us. But what I have to say may not concern her or Judah."

A sudden stab of pain made Hannah wince.

"Mama?"

"It's all right," Hannah told them as she wriggled her body into a more comfortable position.

"You've heard from Aunt Chana again, haven't you," Minya declared.

"That's trouble, plenty of trouble if Papa finds out," Shana added.

"Well, Papa is not going to find out — yet. That is why we must talk."

Hannah wriggled again and once more shifted her position as she reached for the letter.

"Yes, Minya. Your Aunt Chana thinks it is time we left for America. And you are right, Shana, it is plenty of trouble if your father knows that his sister still insists that we leave. But he has to know because I have made up my mind that we are going to go and we cannot go without him. The worry is that I do not know either how to tell him we must go or what would convince him enough to think it was his idea to go in the first place. Your father is a very stubborn and proud man, you know."

"Oh, we know that, Mama. Papa yells and screams a lot," Gissia answered.

A moment or two of silence passed until Gissia spoke again.

"America, Mama? All of us? For good?"

"Yes, Gissia. America. For good. All of us. Your Papa included. But not tonight."

"We have friends, Mama," Gissia persisted. "There's Papa's business, this house, our cousins, uncles, and aunts. There's Judah and Dinah. Do we just pack up and go and leave everyone else behind? My God, Mama! America is at the other end of the world. What will we do there? Do they speak Russian there? Yiddish? German?"

"Sssh," Hannah interrupted. "We don't have time to argue. This land is ours. True. But only because we have lived on it for a long time. But this country is not for us. Chana is right. Terri-

[36]

ble things are in store for us if we remain. I know it. I can feel it. God forbid, the Czar should lose the war — an impossibility, I know — but suppose he does lose? Who do you think will be blamed? The Jews, of course. And who among us will be blamed the most? Your Papa and his brothers. And do you know why? I shall tell you why. Because they will say that the Shapiros sold them poisoned meat that made the army so sick it could not fight. Treason, they will scream! Listen to me, my children. If it is not that, it will be something else and soon. And this time not even the Jews of Krolevets will escape. Maybe then your Papa will wake up and do something — if it is not already too late. One more thing. I am not trying to alarm you needlessly. You know what it is like to be Jewish in Russia. But you must know the hard truth. We shall go to America. Somehow, we shall convince your father to join us. In the meantime, we shall begin to prepare ourselves."

"How, Mama?" Gissia asked for all of them.

"First of all, I want you three to promise me since you are the oldest ones that if something should happen to me — if I should die tonight —"

"Mama!"

"If I should die tonight," Hannah continued, "you must promise me that you will take all the children and go to America whether your Papa goes or not."

"Mama! How can we do that!"

"Promise me! And don't worry. If you tell your Papa that you are leaving, do you think he is going to let you go alone? Of course not. He'll go along to make sure you get there."

"We promise."

"Good. Now, Minya. Get some paper, pen, and ink. I want

[37]

you to write a letter to Chana. I shall talk and you shall write. And remember, not a word to anyone. Is that clear?"

"Yes, Mama!"

Minya returned with paper, pen, and ink. Hannah began:

"First the date, Minya — October 16, 1904."

"I know, Mama."

"Now write, 'My dearest Chana:

" 'Your latest letter came a few days ago. I keep it near me, under my pillow. I feel close to you that way. Benjamin does not want to know about your letters. But soon he is going to have to do something. I have made up my mind to leave here, and God willing, come to New York for good. I told Gissia, Minya, and Shana this today. I made them promise certain things. Of course, I shall not go without my husband and all of our children. How this will be accomplished, I do not know. I think maybe conditions will decide for us. It will not be tomorrow, exactly. Do not be impatient. We shall come. In the meantime, perhaps you and Samuel can talk this over and help us decide what would be the best way to leave Russia and arrive safely in America. We are a large family. There is much to be done. Who will have the house? Who will buy the business? I do not know yet how these things are possible. If I know my husband, he will not want to leave, but if he is forced to leave, he will not want to come to America a victim, without a kopek, dependent on the charity of others — you, for example. He will want to leave with dignity, not flee like a dog with his tail between his legs. If you have any suggestions as to the best means of travel and what preparations will involve us both (you and us), do not hesitate to write. Perhaps you can find out about ships and berths and the costs of these things. There is little we can do about these things now and still keep Benjamin

[38]

from raging. So for the time being, do this for me and the day will come when we shall see each other again. How long has it been? Ten years? Fifteen years? I cannot remember. Soon, Chana. Soon, we shall all be together again, in America. God bless you. Yours, Hannah S.' ''

Hannah winced again. This time the pain was sharper and longer.

"Minya. You will see to it that the letter is posted tomorrow. Shana. I would like you to look over the babies' winter clothes. See that they are in good repair. It seems to me they have been handed down enough. Maybe you can make some new things for them — for travel. And when you finish that —''

"Listen!" Gissia exclaimed. "The bells! The church bells!"

"Never mind the bells," Hannah gasped.

☙ SIX ❧

"Listen!" someone shouted. "The bells! They have seen the train!"

A low murmur rose from the crowd. The members of the official party became more animated, shuffling about, shifting their weight from one foot to the other with restless anticipation. Some of them leaned far over the edge of the platform, peering into the dark distance, discovering, as yet, nothing. Suchenko was shoved accidently from behind and nearly fell off the platform. He saved himself by clinging to his own bell-ringer, ringing the bell violently in the process.

"Suchenko sees the train, too," someone else boomed. Again

[39]

everyone squinted into the distance. But there was only track, no train.

"What time is it now, Benjamin?" Hilya wanted to know with a hint of impatience.

"Why? What difference does it make? Must you be someplace else? Like maybe the widow Gilinsky's place. Ha! You think I do not know about your escapades. I think, Hilya, you had better find yourself a nice bride before the widow's other two lovers cut your throat."

Hilya laughed. "You are too cautious, Benjamin. Life is short enough. I'm not ready for the marriage bed. So what is wrong with being a Casanova?"

Benjamin and Tevya laughed at Hilya's estimation of himself, shaking their heads in amused disbelief. Benjamin looked at his watch and announced the time. "It is five minutes before six."

"The train is an hour late," Tevya observed.

"What does it matter?" Benjamin replied. "So the train is an hour late — maybe two hours late. Maybe it will never get here at all. Now that you know the time, does it matter?"

Benjamin had mixed feelings about the arrival of a railroad line with a stop in Krolevets. He liked the idea that he could go to Konotop or Bakhmach by rail instead of by wagon. It was a convenience for all of them personally and probably good for business. What he did not like was the fact that Krolevets would no longer be insulated from the outside world — from trouble. Strangers would be coming to Krolevets now by train. It would be easy. Who would they be? Why would they come? What would they bring? Whom would they visit? They could be someone's relatives or friends. But then again, they could be anyone — not a relative or a friend, but a troublemaker. There were plenty of those in Russia. And sooner or later they would

[40]

find Krolevets. The train would make it so. Benjamin was not sure he liked the coming changes.

"Of course the time matters," Hilya replied testily. "On such important occasions as this, it is nice to know how fast the day is going and if what we are waiting for will be able to catch the fleeing hours before it is tomorrow."

"Ah, my brother is a philosopher," Benjamin laughed. "You missed your calling, Hilya. You are a thinker. Perhaps you should have been a rabbi. But then again, rabbis do not have time for widowed ladies."

"The day is moving faster than the train," Hilya went on, ignoring his brother's needling.

"Do you think the Czar will really be on the train?" Tevya wondered aloud as if to change the subject.

"One never knows about Nikki," Hilya responded. "If the Czar thinks the train is a toy, he'll be on it."

"Nikki? Since when have you been on such familiar terms with the Czar?" Benjamin inquired.

"Well! What do you think? Yes or no? Czar or no Czar?"

If Benjamin answered his brother, no one heard it. As he opened his mouth, a great roar leaped out of the throng in greeting to two sharp sour blasts of a train whistle.

And there it was, idling stock-still, having materialized suddenly from out of nowhere, or so it seemed, about a half mile away. Two small lanterns were vibrating a low yellowish light on either side of the cowcatcher. The headlamp, centered on the head of the boiler up front, threw a dim beam down the track toward the station. Smoke and steam poured out of the top, sides, and bottom of the locomotive. From where the Shapiros stood, the engine looked like a breathless, perspiring monster pawing the ground, trying to make up its mind

[41]

whether to charge or not.

"Look at that!" Benjamin boomed. "It's an hour late and stops!"

"They have to clear the tracks first," Tevya noted. "Look at those crazy peasants over there. They are all over the rails. How do they expect the train to move?"

"Maybe it wouldn't be a bad idea if it did move," Hilya joked. "A few muzhiks less couldn't hurt. No one would even know the train had run over them."

"Something is clearing those tracks in a hurry. Look at those muzhiks fall down."

"They aren't falling down. They are being knocked down! Oh! I can see them now. Soldiers! Soldiers with rifles and bayonets! They are running down the track."

"What's going on?"

"I don't like the looks of this," Benjamin said.

The night began to close in. A cold wind snapped at the faces in the crowd as it swept the tracks from the north. The dull locomotive lights began to glow brighter. The train began to move. It gave a loud blast of its whistle and picked up speed. As it drew closer, they could see soldiers (some twenty or twenty-five of them fully armed and wearing rolled field blankets) hanging on to the cowcatcher. It was obvious that the train would not stop at Krolevets. It continued to pick up speed and rolled by the surprised and disappointed official party on the platform.

"Look at that!" Hilya exclaimed. "One, two, three, four, five, six, seven, eight, nine, ten — ten cars full of soldiers — troops. There must be five hundred of them. Where did they come from?"

"From Moscow. Where else?"

[43]

"But why?" Tevya insisted on knowing. "They are going in the wrong direction. The war is in Siberia, not in Kiev!"

"Did anyone see the Czar?"

"Who could tell?"

"It might not be a bad thing if they all got off at the next station," Hilya decided.

"Konotop? Why?"

"They would be very good for business. Imagine! Five hundred more hungry soldiers to feed. It would keep us all busy for God knows how long. You, Benjamin, for sure, and Uncle Ara. Perhaps Tevya and I could do a little business on the side."

"And what about Uncle Simon?" asked Benjamin. "He too would be very busy. He would be making bagels until he turned into one."

They all laughed. Uncle Simon — Simon Krichefsky, Simon the bagelmaker — was their mother's brother. The hard doughy bread rings he made were a great favorite everywhere, especially in his speck of a village, Abrijilki. Simon paid particular attention to the troops garrisoned not a mile from Abrijilki. He did not want the soldiers anywhere near him and the villagers, all of whom were Jewish. To keep them away he went to them. He would load up his small broken-down cart and pull it like a horse to the garrison. There he would give away his bagels by the dozens, freely. Simon never took any money from the soldiers — not that they would have paid him. He refused payment before anyone stole a bagel and in that way kept his self-respect.

"For the Czar," he would say aloud. And to himself he would say, "To hell with the Czar! Long live Simon Krichefsky!"

The soldiers would not have harmed the gentle old widower,

physically, despite his fears and instinct for survival. They liked him. They showed their friendliness by supplying Simon with flour they stole from a Jewish miller in another shtetl. Simon and the miller were old friends. He would repay the miller's loss with bagels from his ovens and corned beef wheedled out of his nephew Benjamin. It was not a bad arrangement as far as Simon and the miller were concerned. No one got hurt. And Simon never failed to remind the miller of his "connections," adding, "the next time the soldiers steal a bag of flour, let them take a little extra — it would not be so terrible." And the miller would retort, "For a few more slices of corned beef — maybe."

"Well," Benjamin sighed, "that's that for the train. I suppose there will be others. But I shall tell you something, my dear brothers. If they mean to use the train to move troops in and out of here, it will be very good for business, but it will be very bad for Krolevets. Some soldiers, a few soldiers, are all right. We have always had them, and I know how to deal with them. But a whole army of them right in our yards is not very good. Too many soldiers here will destroy our peace, and in the end they may destroy us."

"Ah! Benjamin. We know what is on your mind. And we sympathize with you," Hilya answered. "But what can be done?"

"What are you talking about?"

"Your daughters, Benjamin. Your daughters. Our nieces. You have a whole army of them. And some of them are a little older than you care to think about. Unmarried too. That is what is on your mind — all those daughters. And they are beautiful girls too. There are none like them anywhere in the district, not even in Chernigov itself. I shouldn't wonder why you are wor-

[45]

ried about all those soldiers." Tevya said his piece with Hilya nodding in agreement.

Benjamin glared at his brothers. They were right and he knew it. How he would have liked to have had nine sons and one daughter rather than the way it turned out — nine daughters and one son. Still, God was good to him. He gave him at least one son, Rachmael. Perhaps He would favor him with another. As for his daughters, God was good to him there too, and he knew that. His daughters were indeed the most beautiful creatures imaginable — bright and perky like Hannah. He would give his life for them. He would move mountains for them. He would see to it that nothing but good things happened to them. Still, another son would hardly upset the order of the universe. What uncertainty!

"Please, God," Benjamin muttered, "do what You think is right."

"Mr. Shapiro! Mr. Shapiro! Wait! I've been looking all over for you. You'd better come home, quickly, right away, hurry."

"What's the matter, Judah? What has happened?"

"It's Mrs. Shapiro! She —"

"Hannah? She what?"

"Mrs. Shapiro had the baby!"

"Mazel tov, Benjamin. Mazel tov!" shouted his brothers, clapping him on the back and looking for a hand to shake.

"So," Benjamin answered. "What is different?" He was almost afraid to ask the baby's sex.

"How is Hannah?"

"Fine."

"Good," Benjamin replied.

"And the baby?" he added.

"Fine also."

[46]

"Good," Benjamin repeated.

"Boy or girl?" he blurted.

Judah looked helplessly at Benjamin's brothers.

"What are you looking at them for? Look at me! Whose baby is it? Theirs or mine?"

"Yours, Mr. Shapiro."

"So?"

"It's a girl."

Benjamin drew himself up to his ramrod-straight height and took a deep breath.

"God did what He thought was right," he said quietly. "Hannah is well — you are sure, Judah?"

"Yes, Mr. Shapiro. Your wife is well."

"Good. And the baby?"

"She is very pretty, as far as I can tell. I saw her, you know."

"No. I did not know," Benjamin replied somewhat vacantly. "A girl, you say?"

"Yes, sir."

Benjamin climbed into Judah's wagon. Judah leaped in after him and grabbed the reins of the two-horse team. A smile blossomed faintly under Benjamin's beard. His eyes glistened in the dusky light.

"I suppose God knew what He was doing. Who am I to question. Do you know, Judah, my boy, it is a blessing for a man to have many sons. But to have so many daughters?" Benjamin's voice trailed off and he shook his head in wonderment as he waved good-bye to his brothers. "But to have so many daughters," he repeated, "there must be a special reason. In the meantime, this girl child will have my mother's name, Dvera. Take me home, Judah."

❦❧ 1905 ❦❧

❂ ONE ❂

The new year was only ten days old and Cera Shapiro, the family's sixteen-year-old bookkeeper, was already two weeks late in closing out last year's accounts book. The babbling excitement in the front room of Shapiro's Delicatessen was hardly noticeable to her as she worked in a back room trying to find some errors in the book. The figures were not adding up.

Cera had worked nearly all through the night trying to straighten out Benjamin's accounts book. The errors were not hers. Benjamin had a bad habit of scribbling figures in the book that only he understood. To make matters even more confusing, he would often pocket receipts, bills, orders, and payments, forgetting to give them to Cera to record.

The only light that flickered from a side window of the long, narrow Shapiro house during the night was the kerosene lamp by which Cera worked. The dark compound, a short walk from Alexander I Square, stood out sharply against a snowy blanket. The great fence, its wide, heavy gate doors locked against intruders by cross timbers and chains, hid the various buildings that formed an additional wall around parts of the property — a barn, chicken coop, wagon shed, bath house, woodshed, a lean-to for peat fuel, meat lockers, an ice house, and an outhouse. Typically, there was no well on the property. Drinking water was either drawn from the town well in the center of the square or purchased from a traveling service that brought large barrels of water weekly and removed the empty barrels. Water for every other purpose came from the river below. The front of the otherwise gray, unpainted, wood-and-stucco house faced the enclosed yard. It was protected by a clump of chestnut trees that grew like weeds for miles around. The back of the house served as one wall of the compound, its long row of shuttered windows locked day and night. A dirt path led around the back to an orchard of pear trees, a good-size vegetable garden, a pine grove, and the Jewish cemetery. The whole of the compound stood on a slight knoll that overlooked the pleasant Seim River Valley.

As Cera worked, looking for the error, more snow silently fell. A goat wandered around the yard while the two guard dogs, Dobermans named Fritzie and Hansie, sniffed the night and barked once or twice. The remainder of the livestock — a flock of geese, some chickens, a family of ducks up from the river, a couple of cows, some horses, and one sheep — were restless but quiet. Other than Cera, the family slept on.

Cera managed to get a few hours of sleep. She arose early with everyone else and took her arithmetical problems to the delicatessen where she continued to work.

The frenzy in the delicatessen's front room carried through the heavy door and almost drowned out the clacking noise of Cera's counting machine, an ancient abacus that had belonged to her grandfather, Rachmael. She could hear Tevya's high-pitched voice cry out, "Who's next?" She knew just where her other uncle, Hilya, would be — at the counter slicing meat and sampling everything he sliced. Their part-time counterman, Sasha Dubrovsky, would be working today. It was that kind of a busy day.

"When the tax collector comes tomorrow, Papa," Cera had scolded her father earlier that morning, "what will you show him? Accounts that only you can read? Do you know what he

[53]

will do, Papa? He will count the buttons on your coat and multiply by one hundred, and that will be the tax you will pay! Five hundred rubles! You have five buttons."

"I shall not wear a coat," Benjamin said with some amusement. Ah, he thought, how did I get along in this world before?

"Five hundred rubles, Papa! Are you listening? That is twenty times more than you would have to pay had you put the figures down right in the first place as I told you. Remember the new system? Papa, you do not have five hundred rubles cash to give to a tax collector!"

"Ah, yes. Out with the old system. In with the new system. Make way for the new. Can it be fixed, Cera?" Benjamin plaintively asked.

"I suppose so, Papa. I am trying," Cera said with exasperation. "If I do not fix it they will send you to Siberia and that will be the end of you. And I shall miss you," she added.

Benjamin burst out laughing and Cera flung her arms around him and kissed him.

"Who can add and subtract this mess with that noise out there?" she asked.

Cera unhooked herself from her father and returned to the abacus. Benjamin went back to the crowd in the front room.

The din had become agitated, unbearable. Cera went out front. She had little difficulty seeing her father in the middle of the crowded room. Not only because he was a head taller than everyone else, but because he stood straight as a stick while the others were crooked and bent from their weary lives, burdens, and prayer books.

"Look at them," Benjamin used to say in the synagogue. "Look at them. What bad posture they all have. Too much praying. Too much reading. Too much bending over. No wonder why most of them will never stand straight again."

When Benjamin turned his face toward her, Cera saw an ashen, vacant look she had never seen on it before. It was as if life had drained out of it. She thought he seemed suddenly to bend a little — a slight stoop — as the old Jews of whose posture he was always so critical. His dazed, blank, colorless countenance told her that their lives somehow had unalterably changed.

"What is it, Papa?"

"Fifteen hundred," he said. "Fifteen hundred." Benjamin shook his head to clear his disbelief. He seemed to come alive again.

"Fifteen hundred what?"

"Suchenko just brought terrible news, Cera. He received a wire with information that Russia has suffered a great defeat in a place called Port Arthur. Have you heard of it? No matter. But that is not what is so terrible. What is terrible is that as soon as the defeat was known there were strikes all over."

"Let's go in the back, Papa. It's a little quieter there. I can hear you better." Cera pulled him by the arm into the room and shut the door.

"Thousands marched to the palace in St. Petersburg the other day," Benjamin went on. "They yelled 'Free press! Free speech!' and things like that. Crazy! That's when it happened."

"For God's sake, Papa, that's when what happened?"

"The Czar ordered his guard to fire on the marchers. They did! They killed fifteen hundred of them just like that." Benjamin snapped his fingers. "Russians they killed. Not Jews! Russians! How many Jews live in St. Petersburg? A handful? And then Suchenko tells us (and this part was in the telegram) that the government said the troops fired on Jewish agitators; all

[56]

Jews, the officials claim, because they could not admit they killed Russians! Bloody Sunday, Suchenko called it, I think."

"What will happen, Papa?"

"Wait, there is more. There are riots and disorders all over. Not here in Krolevets, but in the big cities. Suchenko said that he expected troops to disembark at his station momentarily. Can you imagine! Troops here in Krolevets! But worse still, the navy in Odessa has mutinied. They are blaming it on rotten meat. Our meat!"

"Why our meat? How can that be?"

"Our meat because they have been getting it secondhand from the Ninth Army Corps Quartermaster — our customer. I've known about that for weeks."

Benjamin sagged in his chair. What little color had returned to his face left it again.

"Simienko dropped by also. I asked him how much truth there was to all of this. After all, he must know something. He's an army officer. He said it was all true. 'The country is in a state of revolution.' Those were his exact words. But then I looked around and I did not see any revolution. Everything looked the same as always. Go outside, Cera. See for yourself. It's the same old Krolevets — quiet, peaceful. Same trees, buildings."

Cera did not budge. She waited for her father to continue.

"Simienko told me about the mutiny and that the Ninth Army Corps Quartermaster, Colonel Timiroff — you know him, the short, wide, squat fellow — sold meat rations to the Odessa naval units after we had sold the goods to him. He kept the money for himself! Simienko is an old friend; at least that is what I thought until now. He said not to worry because Timiroff was arrested and will be shot. But then he said something to make me worry more. I think he was trying to warn me."

"Warn you? About what?"

"'Shapiro,' he said, 'we all know and like you. We respect you. I knew your father and liked him. I am old enough to be your father, you know. I have heard it said that your grandfather would have been sainted had he been of the Russian faith. You are an honest man from a good and venerable family. You are also a first-class provisioner of quality goods (that was nice to hear, Cera, very nice) even though you are a Jew!' He said that! Can you imagine! Simienko has done much for us over the years. Never once has he concerned himself out loud with whether or not we were Jews. His own granddaughter, Maria, and our Gissia have been best of friends for years. Is that not so? Now, all of a sudden this has changed. Even though I am a Jew! he said."

"Papa, let's go home. You do not look well. You are talking too much."

"Please, Cera. I am not finished. And then Simienko hoped that we were not involved in the revolution politically, or in 'political agitation' like all the rest of the Jews. Who is he talking about, Cera? What politics? Shapiros are not political. He knows that. None of us. Ever!"

"There has been talk, Papa. Some of the young people —"

Benjamin vaulted out of his chair, wild-eyed with disbelief and anger. Who would dare upset the delicate harmony of their peace (the Jewish peace of Krolevets) that had lasted for a hundred or more years?

"What young people?" he roared. "You? Gissia? Minya? Shana? Who?"

"None of us, Papa. Don't upset yourself over nothing."

[58]

"Upset myself! Over nothing! It's that damn train," he bellowed. "Outsiders come in here now very easily and quickly with new ideas, stirring up trouble. Jew, Gentile — what's the difference — troublemakers all!"

"Please, Papa. Let's go home."

"I do not remember riots, marching malcontents, and so many dead Russians shot by other Russians. Fifteen hundred! I cannot remember a single revolution! The Czar must have gone mad. Crazy! We are going to lose this war. Maybe we have already lost it. Russia will explode from the humiliation! And then they will blame the Jews. They always did when there was trouble. Soon that trouble will come to Krolevets. It will come by train. The trouble will not stop to find out who is good or bad, who is worthy or unworthy, political or non political. The trouble will look to kill Jews. That's all. Kill Jews! That is how the world and Russia solves problems, by killing Jews. It will never be different. Church bells will ring and Jews will die!"

Cera had never heard her father talk of these things with such passion. A sudden chill overcame her. She tightened the shawl she was wearing for more warmth. And Benjamin went on.

"Listen to me, Cera. I remember the pogroms after Czar Alexander was murdered by Gentiles and how the Jews suffered for it. I can still hear those church bells. They were everywhere in the air all at once — all over the district, all over Chernigov. And when they would stop there would be dead or crippled Jews in every town, on every road. We thought it would never end. Sure, they caught the murderers and hanged them. But they still blamed it on the Jews. Incredible! But true! We must —"

Benjamin was cut off by the shattering noise of breaking

[59]

glass, screams, and tumult. A huge rock had been heaved through the front window of the delicatessen. A minute or so later Suchenko and Major Simienko burst out of the terrified crowd into the back room. Tevya, bleeding from a cut on the side of his head, and Hilya, unhurt, were right behind them.

"Shapiro! Good friend! Citizen! It was a mistake! Those hooligans were not supposed to touch this establishment. It was a mistake! Believe us!"

Benjamin stared with shock at his bleeding brother. Speechless, he turned and looked at Suchenko and Simienko. He did not hear their seeming apology, only the peal of the bells from the Church of Our Saviour a few doors away.

❧ TWO ❧

The impact of defeat at Port Arthur (a place most Russians had never heard of and now wondered about) had hardly worn off when disaster struck again — twice in two months. In February, assassins struck in Moscow. They murdered the Czar's uncle, Grand Duke Sergei. In March, as the Easter season approached Christendom, and the Jews prepared to celebrate the Passover holiday commemorating their ancient deliverance from Egypt, a badly mauled Russian army was driven from Mukden, Manchuria and surrendered to the forces of Japan.

It was springtime. The winter snows still deep and wet in the north had all but melted into the muddy black ooze of the Ukraine. With news of the surrender, a mortal chill had fallen on the land.

"We cannot let them succeed," exclaimed Czar Nicholas II

over and over again, unable to comprehend the strikes at home or the war in the Pacific. No one knew if he was really talking about the revolutionaries in his own capital city, St. Petersburg, who despite their one thousand five hundred dead continued to pressure the government and die, or the military forces of Japan, who walloped his forces at will.

"We cannot tolerate civil disorder and disobedience," the Czar lectured his war cabinet. "To put a stop to it we must have a decisive victory." He ordered one of the world's most powerful naval squadrons, the Imperial Russian Baltic Sea Fleet, all the way to Japanese waters. "If we cannot have them on land, we'll have them at sea."

The fleet sailed with deadly purpose and never came back. Neither did ten thousand Russian sailors. The Japanese Navy caught the Russians on a beautiful May morning and destroyed them. The war was over.

"Do something!" cried the incredulous Czar to his ministers. They did. They accepted an invitation from American President Theodore Roosevelt to meet with him at Portsmouth, New Hampshire, to work out a suitable peace treaty with Japan. Roosevelt would be awarded the Nobel Peace Prize. Japan would go on a forty-year military spree in Asia. Sulking Russia would be convulsed by riots and strikes within a month of the September signing of the Treaty of Portsmouth. These spreading disorders would be put down by wonderful promises of reform that never materialized. The government, intending no reform, blamed the Jews.

"Did I not tell you this would happen," Benjamin wearily told Hannah.

"You told me?" Hannah retorted testily.

A month after the peace treaty with Japan was signed, in October, the strikers and rioters, prodded by the Czar, turned their frustration on the Jews. Six hundred and ninety attacks were mounted against the Jews of the Ukraine. Half of these contrived assaults occurred in the district of Chernigov which, strangely enough, was populated by fewer Jews than any area in the "Pale of Settlement." Not even sleepy Krolevets escaped.

◙ THREE ◙

The portent of things to come happened shortly after the Russian army went down under the gun of Japanese General Iwao Oyama at Mukden. It came as a knock on the Shapiro door, near midnight, Saturday, April 2.

"Shapiro! Benjamin! Are you there? Wake up!"

"Who's out there?" Judah Labe wanted to know, his voice rising to be heard above the barking Dobermans.

Judah and Dinah had moved in with the Shapiros. Hannah had insisted on it after Judah was pulled from the wagon in front of the delicatessen and beaten up.

"That'll teach the Jew-boy a lesson he won't soon forget," one of the attackers remarked as he and several others left Judah half-conscious in the mud. Judah had never seen any of his assailants before. Neither had anyone else. They were strangers — peasant youths from some other town. "They came by train," Benjamin had announced. "And they left by train. Who knows who they are, where they come from, or who sent them?"

"Who's out there?" Judah asked again.

"Cherniskov, the shoemaker. Let me in."

[62]

Judah looked through a crack. He was satisfied that it was indeed Cherniskov the shoemaker and that he was alone. He let him in.

"Hurry! Take me to Benjamin. Wake him up! Hurry!"

Benjamin was already awake. The barking dogs had jarred him from his sleep. Hannah was with him. The children were beginning to stir. Gissia and Ita followed their parents into the large kitchen. Benjamin calmly threw a few blocks of peat into the cast-iron stove to take the chill out of the air. Cera, Shana, Minya, and Rochlia all staggered in half-asleep. Rachmael wandered in rubbing his eyes. The little ones — Rivka, Mera, Feiga, and Dvera — stayed in their beds. Dinah fussed over them.

"Benjamin, Mrs. Shapiro," the shoemaker began, "we have been friendly neighbors all of our lives. We have lived together in peace. I have made for you the best boots in Russia. You have kept my wife and me from starving many a winter and took nothing in return. I am old and we are childless. Your children have been our children from a distance. We are not all monsters. So this I do for you."

"Do what?"

"I am coming to that. Tomorrow morning — it is already to-morrow morning — at first light, you will hear the bells for Chernigov, Konotop, Bakhmach, Nezhin, Glukhov, Starodub, Pochep, Surazh, Novozybkov, and Novgorod-Seversk. . . . "

"I know all of that, Leonid. You do not have to recite all the towns with churches," Benjamin replied impatiently. "I also know that tomorrow is Palm Sunday, an important religious holiday for you. So why not bells?"

"Yes. Yes. An important holiday," the shoemaker repeated. "But for you and the Jews of Chernigov it may be the last day

[63]

of your lives. A great plan has been hatched to murder you all in your beds. The government says that you Jews are revolutionaries, agitators, anarchists, and murderers, responsible for all the murders, riots, shootings, and military defeats!"

"Impossible! Insanity!" Benjamin hissed.

"Kishinev!" was all that Hannah could think of to say.

"You are in danger, Benjamin. All of you. A trainload of toughs has already been unloaded at the station. They are there now waiting for the signal."

"How do you know this, Leonid, my friend?"

"I saw them myself. I made some boots for my sister's children in Konotop. I brought them there myself yesterday. I took the train. I returned tonight. And when I got off the train, there they were. I do not know how many. It was too dark to tell. Suchenko was there watching over his station. He was very nervous. He saw me, told me what was what and sent me to warn you. He is your friend, Benjamin."

"That's possible," said Benjamin half aloud, "very possible."

"We are wasting time," Cherniskov said. "Everyone must come to my house now. It will be safer there. I do not think the gang will come out here. But one never knows. It will be light soon. Hurry!"

"I am not going," Benjamin announced. "Judah and I shall remain here. There isn't room enough for everybody in Cherniskov's cottage. On second thought, all of the men will remain here. And that includes Rachmael!"

"You cannot do this to us," Hannah argued. "You will all be killed."

"Nobody will be killed. We shall be safely hidden in the barn. Peasants, if that is who they are, do not burn down

[64]

barns. They burn down houses, not barns. They do not look for people in barns, only animals. We shall be safe there."

No amount of further argument or persuasion could move Benjamin. "This is my house and the house of my father before me. I will not be chased from it. I will not leave it empty."

A half hour later, Hannah, Dinah, and the brood were safely tucked away in the house of their compassionate Gentile neighbor. Benjamin, Judah, and Rachmael stayed behind, buried in a pile of damp straw in the barn. There they waited for doomsday.

The dawn came. An orange glow flooded the eastern sky. The day promised to be unseasonably warm. Feodor Korbeyev pulled on the bellrope of Krolevets's Church of Our Saviour with more muscular purpose than he knew he had. The sonorous music rolled across the town and mingled with the other rich and resonant bongs awakening the district of Chernigov. It was Palm Sunday.

With the soaring bells pounding in their ears and a rousing night of vodka swilling taking its toll in their bellies, a ragged mob lurched and stumbled across Alexander I Square screaming, "Zid! Zid! Zid! Jew! Jew! Jew!" They attacked the synagogue, led by the schoolteacher Yuri Malinikov, who had promised Rabbi Sarchefsky that one day he would "see the truth and the light."

"Do you hear something, Papa?" frightened Rachmael wanted to know.

"Yes, Rachmael, I hear something. Shhh."

In ten minutes it was finished. Except for two or three who had passed out in drunken stupors and lay at the entrance of the synagogue, the mob had vanished. They had done their

[65]

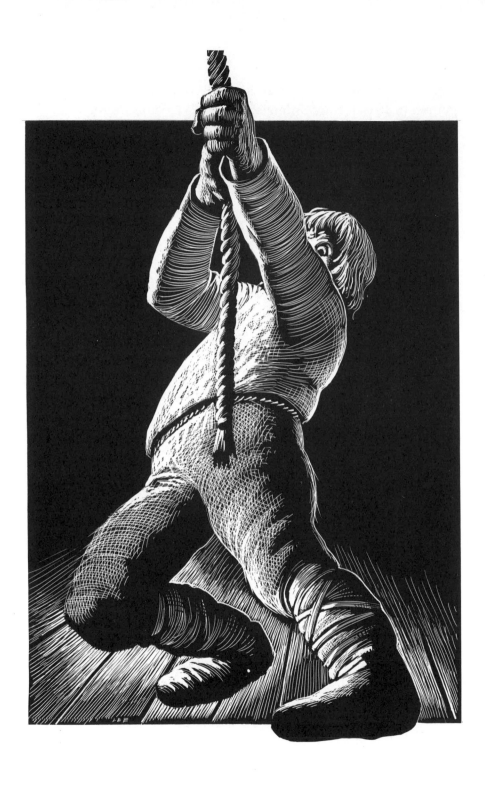

work like a swarm of locusts defoliating a corn field. Rabbi Sarchefsky, who had been warned too, had elected to stay in his holy house, the captain of a sinking ark. The mob, in its fury, swept past him without seeing him as it went about its vile business of breaking every window, hurling the furniture and furnishings, holy books, articles, and Torahs into a bonfire outside. Everything was burned.

The ashes were swept up the following day and carefully shoveled into a coffin. The lid was nailed tightly into place and a great funeral procession began. Krolevets had never seen the likes of it before. Some two thousand or more Jews of the town followed the coffin to the cemetery. Benjamin Shapiro walked at the head of the procession with the rabbi and several others. Directly behind him were his brothers. Somewhere in the line were Hannah and the children. There, at the cemetery, the box containing the ashes of the holy treasures of the Jews of Krolevets (some of them four and five hundred years old, from Spain, Germany, and Poland, and other places in the west whence came the ancestors of Krolevets's Jews) was buried. And the weeping multitude recited the timeless, age-old Hebrew prayer for the dead:

Yisgadal v'yskadash sh'me rabbo. . . .

On the Tuesday evening that followed, Jews sat down to feast and remind themselves of how Moses delivered them from Egyptian bondage in the days of the Pharaohs. It was the first night of Passover.

In the Shapiro household, young Rachmael stood at the crowded table preparing to recall those ancient historic events of Hebrew slavery and Hebrew freedom with the traditional questions. And true to ancient custom, Benjamin reclined on a

[67]

spray of pillows at the head of the table instead of being seated in a chair. The family nervously began to celebrate in an uncertain atmosphere.

"Why is this night," Rachmael began tentatively. "Why is this night different from all other nights?"

He stopped momentarily. His head jerked up with alarm.

"The bells!" someone said softly. "The church bells."

"We will continue," Benjamin commanded. "I cannot hear the bells. Neither can any of you. Last Sunday we feared for our lives. Nothing happened. Not to us personally. They wrecked the synagogue. That's all. Just a building. No one was harmed. And no one will be harmed. Go on, Rachmael. But just in case, Hilya will go outside and listen and watch for a while. Judah, you will go too."

Hilya and Judah walked around outside. The animals seemed restless. The Dobermans paced up and down on the ends of their chains. The two men saw nothing. All they heard was the frantic ringing of the bells. Rachmael went on. But for the rest of the night, the bellringer, drunk since Palm Sunday, gleefully worked on the tattered nerves of the Jews; terrible anxiety had left them shaken and jumpy over what would come next. They had only to wait a few days.

Good Friday, a day commemorating the crucifixion of Jesus Christ, a Jew from Nazareth, began and ended quietly. The stubborn and courageous Jews of Krolevets spent Friday night and Saturday in their wrecked synagogue. It was still Passover. There, they tried to bring the shell back to life, praying from their personal books and memories. A new Torah would not arrive until August.

Easter Sunday dawned like Palm Sunday a week earlier. An

orange ball slowly lifted itself into the clear eastern sky and began to light up the day. In Alexander I Square, every Jewish shop but two was smashed and vandalized to the mad rhythm of Korbeyev and his bells as the Easter service reeled in the hollow of the sanctuary of the Church of Our Saviour, deafened by the noise above.

"I do not understand," Hannah exclaimed. "Berkhan and Morozovski, the photographers and Shapiro's Delicatessen — not a scratch?"

"A miracle, Hannah! A miracle!" Benjamin replied, looking up at the sky. He knew better. The broken window had not been replaced. The front of the store was boarded up. There was little damage anyone could do to the shop short of burning it down. And if they did that then the whole square would go up in smoke in no time. Still, he knew better. No one broke into the shop to vandalize it. And he knew why.

In the week between Palm Sunday and Easter Sunday an arrangement had been made. "Shapiro is rich," Chief of Police Tartazov told Suchenko. "Does he not spread his generosity here and there?"

"He is not rich in cash, Nikolai. It is only a few kopeks here and there. It makes for friendship between him and us. That's all."

"Nonsense! You mean between him and you, not him and us. Perhaps if he were approached to increase his contribution to the Candle Fund. . . ."

"You know about that?"

"Do you think the Jew would be pleased if he knew that *you*, Suchenko, were the Candle Fund? Do you think the priest would be pleased?"

[69]

"But Nikolai, what you suggest is all right in some places and for some people. But not here in Krolevets with Shapiro. He and his family belong here. They are respected and honorable. They have connections. They have —"

"I have heard enough," Tartazov declared, cutting off Gregor Suchenko's plea on behalf of the Shapiros. "As far as the Shapiros being respected and honorable, belonging here and having connections — they are Jews; they do not belong here and never have. And with regards to connections — bah! These are new times. Soon he will be without connections."

"What do you propose, Nikolai?"

"You will approach Shapiro to increase his contribution to the Candle Fund by, let us say, one ruble a week. As an accommodation we might be able to afford him some protection from the hooligans the government sends down here. What do they call them — oh, yes, the Black Hundreds. Two rubles might be necessary to protect his house, three rubles his family, and so on. There is precedent for such an arrangement. I have already reached an agreement with Berkhan and Morozovski. Now they can take pictures to their hearts' content. Work it out, Suchenko, and maybe I shall let you keep your few kopeks."

Benjamin sputtered and fumed. Suchenko apologized, begged forgiveness for such a criminal act and advised Benjamin to pay, assuring him that there would come a better day for everyone. Benjamin paid. He had bought time and safety, for how long he had no idea. Maybe that better day would come. Things were changing too fast for him to understand. Maybe Tartazov would be found out and shot for extortion. Maybe not. Maybe it would not be a crime to extort money from Jews. Benjamin shivered and slept little.

[70]

❧ FOUR ❧

Suchenko reached across the counter and handed Benjamin the telegram he had received only moments before. Benjamin wiped his hands on his apron and read:

12 JUNE 1905 BROOKLYN NEW YORK
RECEIVED KROLEVETS CHERNIGOV OBLAST RUSSIA
BENJAMIN/HANNAH SHAPIRO
LEAVE NOW STOP AT ONCE STOP DANGEROUS STOP
PLEASE ADVISE CHANA W.

"What will you advise, Benjamin?"

Benjamin did not rage at the prospect of leaving Russia as he once had. He was tired. He was more absent-minded of late. He even forgot to remove his apron before climbing into the wagon to go home. He looked at Gissia and the others who had joined them at the kitchen table — Minya, Shana, Cera, Ita, and Rochlia.

"Where are the rest of you?" he asked.

Rochlia skipped out and rounded up Rachmael, who was helping Judah load a wagon with sides of beef destined for an army unit in Shostka, a few miles north of Krolevets. Rivka and Mera drifted in from the hen house with a basket of eggs. Dinah appeared with sleeping Dvera in her arms and Feiga pulling at her skirt.

Hannah gathered her children around her. Benjamin remained seated while everyone stood, backing off a bit, waiting for him to speak.

[71]

"Please," he began, "a glass of tea. I cannot think without a glass of tea."

"Maybe a glass of warm goat's milk would be better, Benjamin."

"All right, goat's milk." Benjamin had forgotten about his ulcer ever since the train had begun running through Krolevets. There was so much else to think about, it never occurred to him to think that much about himself. Now the pains were returning. Hannah could tell. Benjamin winced slightly and gently rubbed his stomach. The goat's milk would make him feel better.

"It is not easy," he said, his voice wavering.

"Nothing is easy anymore, Benjamin," Hannah said with obvious impatience.

Gissia stepped forward out of the solid group and handed her father a warm glass of goat's milk. "Papa," she began, "when was the last time you spoke with Major Simienko? Maria Simienko will not speak to me anymore. We have been friends for as long as I can remember."

"Natasha, Simienko's daughter, the unmarried one, old enough to be my grandmother," Cera interrupted, "called me a Jew-bitch. No one ever called me that before!"

Benjamin looked up puzzled from his glass of warm goat's milk.

"Papa," Minya chimed in, "will any of the children be able to go to a proper school? How much do you think I can teach them? And will I be able to go to a university?"

"Papa." It was Shana's turn. "I am afraid. I have never been afraid before. Every day someone else is beaten up. Soon it will be you and Mama and us. I do not want to go. But I do not want to stay."

"Papa." Cera spoke again. She fairly spat out the word "papa" as she faced Benjamin. "It is finished!" She waited for Benjamin to react. He did not. "It is not we who must decide. Or you. It is they — the Gentiles — who have decided for us. They do not want us. They never have! We are only fooling ourselves if we think otherwise. Our world is crumbling — our Russian world — and we will die in it if you do not do something soon."

"Papa," said Ita, "if we go to America, we will not be alone. Many have gone before us. Friends of yours and Mama's and ours. There is Aunt Chana and Uncle Samuel and cousins we want to know. There is Uncle David and your own cousins — Uncle Ara's sons, Harry and Carl. I think there are more Shapiros in America than in Krolevets and Konotop together."

"Papa," Rochlia added, "if we do not like America, can we not return to Krolevets?"

"Well! Rachmael! Rivka! Mera! Don't you have something to say too? Maybe now Feiga will speak! And Dvera! Everybody knows what has to be done but me! Do you think this is easy?" he repeated. "Do you think all you have to do is pack a valise and poof you go?"

Benjamin marched out of the kitchen — out of the house — leaving his untouched glass of goat's milk cooling on the table. "We shall wait for you right here," Hannah called after him. "We are not going to move until you make up your stubborn mind to go!"

Benjamin made a quick turn around and stomped back into the kitchen. "What about this house? This property? My business? The store? Judah and Dinah? Where does the money

[74]

come from to make such a voyage? Do you know what you are asking?"

"What about our lives?" Hannah angrily retorted. "Have you no regard for our lives?"

"What about my brothers and my sister? What will become of them?"

"What of your own children, Benjamin? They are the ones that should concern you the most. The rest of the family must decide their own lives. Dinah and Judah too! You cannot live in their lives and they cannot live in ours! You are the head of this household, not the household of everyone else!"

Benjamin stalked out of the house again. "We'll be right here when you get back," Hannah called after him.

Benjamin drifted around the yard aimlessly, passing Judah once or twice without looking at him. Judah had been in his employ about five years, maybe six. He could not remember. He finally wandered down the path to the cemetery where he confronted the graves of his parents.

"What should I do?" he asked. "Hannah is right," he told the gravestone. "I shall not be able to deal with the situation here much longer. Business has not been so good lately. And I do not think it is going to get better. Then what? It may be too late to do anything about anything. Go to America now? Some trip! Give up what we have? Will we have as much in America? Who will we be in America?"

Benjamin meandered around the graveyard reading this gravestone and that, many of them his own forebears. There was a stream of continuity in the generations of Shapiros that taxed and numbed his mind. "Who are we here?" he wondered. "Who have we ever been?"

[75]

For at least seven hundred years, beginning in 1096 A.D. with the undisciplined First Crusade of Walter the Penniless and Peter the Hermit, the forebearers of Benjamin Shapiro had carried variations of the name "Spira" while fleeing forever eastward across Europe from present-day Speyer, Germany, a town on the Rhine River. Spira became Shapiro when the family finally came to rest at the end of the eighteenth century in Chernigov District. Here they had survived and prospered for a little more than one hundred years. Now it was time to go again, not eastward but westward — westward to America.

Benjamin returned to the kitchen. No one had left.

"How do we make such a voyage, Hannah? All of us. It will require documents, papers, permits. It cannot be done overnight. Where does so much money come from? How do we keep it quiet until we are ready? We cannot just run. We'll never get there alive."

"Just tell us, Benjamin, yes or no. We shall worry about the details later. America? Yes or no?"

"Yes."

⚅ FIVE ⚅

Neither Hilya nor Tevya could believe their ears.

"America?"

"America!"

"With eleven children? You must be out of your mind. Why not take a trip to the moon? Foolishness. Do you think things are always going to be this bad in Russia? This is the twentieth century, Benjamin. Why leave? We have all been through hard times before. We have a decent life here, all of us. A good business where so many have nothing. We have respect. Things will improve. America is a wild place. . . ."

"And Russia is a tame place? Please, Hilya, Tevya. Talk sense. Don't talk nonsense. Listen to me. Both of you. I have made up my mind. I do —"

"You mean Hannah made up your mind!"

"I do not want to go. None of us really wants to go. But we must. And that's that!"

"You go. And we'll still be here when you come back."

Benjamin sighed. He did not want words with his brothers.

"I am leaving a hundred lifetimes behind. Hannah does not feel as tied to this place as I feel. I cannot bear to part from you or the dead. This is my home and my life such as it is. But Hannah and I have eleven children. You do not. They can kill me someday and they probably will if we stay. But they will not touch my children. They deserve better. They deserve to live in a place that has no laws against them just because they are Jews; a place where they can all go to school like everyone else, even though they are Jews; a place where they and their children and their children's children will be as safe as anyone else; a place where the danger is the same for Jew and Gentile; a place where they do not smash synagogues by decree because the government says to smash synagogues."

"How do you know they do not smash synagogues on order in America?"

"I do not know. I only assume from all that I have heard. I do not know much about America. I admit this. But the whole world cannot be crazy and ignorant. Everybody is going there."

"Good. Let them go. The more that go there, the better off we'll be here."

[77]

"You two are impossible to talk to. Listen. If Chana and Samuel say come, how bad can it be? I am forty-six years old. I have lived my life. I have already lived thirteen years longer than Papa. I am getting to be an old man. It is time that I had grandchildren. Gissia and Minya and Shana should be married by now. But no! No one here is good enough! Pretty soon it will be too late for them. They say that America is the land of opportunity. Perhaps that includes husbands for my girls. Who knows? Either I do this now while I still have the strength and the children are not yet old like me, or else I must forget the matter. Will you help me?"

"What can we do?"

"Buy me out. Buy the store, the business — the *Gildiya Kupyet* authorization will go with it. I shall see to it. Buy the house, the land, everything."

"The goat too? Do we have to buy the goat? It's the milk from that goat that keeps you alive. How can you go to America without that goat? You will have to drag it with you."

"Please, Hilya, Tevya. Be serious. This is no joking matter. I have some money. I am going to need more. Not much. Just enough to care for thirteen people with a little left over so that we do not arrive in America as paupers. There will be expenses."

"How much will you need? After all, we are not wealthy men. We only work for you," Tevya said.

"Maybe that's why we are not wealthy men," Hilya added, unable to resist the wisecrack.

"Listen, you two. I know you work for me. And I have paid you well just as if you were my partners. We have shared in proportion to our need. We have taken care of each other. I

[78]

also know that you have done a little business of your own on the side. How do I know? Simple. I let you use my wagons. Do you think I do not know these things? You two have done very well for yourselves."

"All right, Benjamin. Give us a figure. What do you need?"

"I cannot give you a figure until Minya finds out what our documents and tickets will cost, and until Cera tells me what the business is worth, what the property is worth, and who knows what else."

Over the past year, Benjamin had grown very dependent on Cera, his bookkeeper, and Minya, his scholar. No one, not even he, had so clear an understanding of the relationship of arithmetic to business as Cera did. And no one seemed to know as much about current Russian affairs as Minya did.

"We have to find out the cost of going from here to there — the train, the ship, food, sleeping somewhere, fees, and documents. Believe me, if I were going alone, I would not bother with all of this. I would walk across the borders when no one would be watching and hide on a ship, steal food, and do whatever else would be necessary to keep alive. It has been done many times. But I have babies and women. Oh, do I have women! Thank God for Rachmael! But he is only eight. I am not asking for the moon. I shall sell out as cheaply as possible so that we may go. All I want to know now is whether or not you will help. Then I shall advise Chana and Samuel that we are coming. And then we shall work out the details."

"What if we refuse?" Tevya asked sharply.

"We shall be unable to go — all of us."

"What if we should counter your figure with a lower offer? After all, you are not in a very good bargaining position. We do

[79]

not want to make it easy for you to leave. We have been . . ." The tears welled up in Hilya's eyes and he was unable to continue.

"Please, no tears. Don't make it more painful than it already is. My offer will be fair. And the only way you will get the certificate is to meet my offer; otherwise I shall seek another way."

Hannah and Benjamin waited about a week before replying to their relatives in New York. They had formulated a rough plan to ensure their safe transit to New York, one they felt they could manage; it was a plan that would not make beggars out of them before they left or upon their arrival in New York. Benjamin insisted. Hannah agreed.

Judah was sent to Uncle Ara in Konotop to tell him that plans were underway to emigrate to America. He had two other tasks as well. Judah was to post a registered letter to Samuel and Chana Weinstein. And he was to send a telegram in *his* name — not in the name of Shapiro — with four words:

PREPARE STOP LETTER TO FOLLOW STOP

Benjamin had decided that Judah should do these things in another town. He did not want to alert Suchenko, the telegrapher, postmaster, and stationmaster, needlessly. Suchenko was proving to be trustworthy in Benjamin's mind. However, he was wary of Suchenko's ties to Police Chief Tartazov.

"The less Gregor Suchenko knows at the moment," Benjamin told everyone, "the safer we shall be. It isn't Suchenko who worries me. It is Tartazov."

The registered letter would not reach New York until late

[80]

August — in two months time. It could not have been plainer:

Dear Chana and Samuel:

We are all fine, healthy, safe, and sound, except for Feiga, of course. Poor Feiga. She still cannot hear or speak. Herschel says that she will always be like that. Anyway, it is necessary to post this from Konotop for reasons that I cannot explain now. It is done. Finished. We are coming. But it is hard to say when. Hilya and Tevya have agreed to help by buying the house, business, and everything we own that we are not taking, even Benjamin's goat! We beg you, if it is at all possible, to do what we cannot do from here. We are afraid to send money for you to use on our behalf. It may never get there. Besides, we do not have that much right now. We have decided that Gissia, Shana, Cera, and Ita will go first and as soon as possible. Gissia is the oldest and she will help prepare our way. Shana sews well and will find work easier than others. So, too, will Cera who has a good business head. Ita gets along well with others. She will be more of a help to her sisters on the long voyage than she will be remaining with us. As for the rest, Minya will show us the way. She studied geography, you know. Everyone else will have their part. But we cannot send Gissia, Shana, Cera, and Ita without arrangements. They are our daughters and we want them to come to you safe and sound. Will you, can you make arrangements for the boat trip? We shall see that they get to the boat with proper documents. Just tell us where and when. We will pay you back when we are settled in America, God willing. Do not send any more telegrams to Krolevets. Do not send any letters to Krolevets that speak of these matters – our leaving. Please send all such letters to Ara Shapiro in Konotop. We await your answer.

Hannah S.''

[81]

While Cera worked on the figures to determine how much the business, house, and other belongings were worth for sale, Minya made a list of the approximate cost of the trip:

Ship tickets for 13 one way @ 80* rubles each	1040 rubles
Passport for 13	5
Police residence permits	20
Travel permits	65
Train tickets, 2nd class coach with reserve seats	400
Miscellaneous	470
Total	2000 rubles

"What is miscellaneous?" Benjamin wanted to know.

"Food. We have to eat, you know. Maybe even sleep someplace before we get on the ship."

"So! Since we do not have the cash for all, then either we all stay or we go a few at a time. Tell me, Minya, how much would it cost if we sent, let's say, four of us?"

Minya made another list:

Ship tickets for 4 one way @ 80 rubles each	320 rubles
Passport for 4	5
Police residence permits	5
Travel permits	25
Train tickets, 2nd class coach with reserve seats	100
Miscellaneous	145
Total	600 rubles

*in 1905–1906, one Russian ruble = $.50 United States currency.

"If Chana and Samuel buy the ship tickets and we do the rest, then all we need is 280 rubles. And this I've got with a little to spare. It's settled. Four will go first. Gissia, the oldest, will be in charge. Shana and Cera will go because maybe they will be able to find work quickly sewing and figuring. If they can do this, then they will be able to help pay whatever debts we have to Chana and Samuel. And Ita will go because she is not backward in talking to people and paving the way."

◘ SIX ◘

The dry hot summer pushed on. Brown dust lay like a cocoa veil over the restless Ukraine. Pamphlets and circulars appeared seemingly out of thin air denouncing the Czar, the entire government, and the privileged.

"Do you see these papers?" Benjamin shouted, waving a fistful of circulars over his head. "They came by train! Nothing but trouble comes by that train!"

The papers fluttered everywhere as Benjamin hurled them at the sky. And they floated to earth exhorting the Russian people to action.

"Free speech! Free press! Free assembly!" the circulars demanded.

"Free religion! What of free religion?" Rabbi Sarchefsky asked while standing in front of Shapiro's still wounded, unrepaired delicatessen window, a pamphlet clenched in his fist. Two or three customers dragged him inside.

"What's the matter with you, rabbi? Are you crazy? Do you

[83]

want to be shot? You have free religion, do you not? Nobody says you cannot be a Jew. Do not ask for something you already have or the Czar will take that away from you too and you will have nothing. Free speech! Free press! Free assembly! What do these things matter to you? You are a Jew. Be thankful you are alive and that you can eat Shapiro's pickles and corned beef."

Judah Labe chased back and forth between his employer, Benjamin Shapiro, and his employer's uncle, Ara Shapiro — between Krolevets and Konotop and back again. He spent half of June, all of July, and most of August seeking some word from New York. He had no interest in America, only Palestine. And Benjamin had promised to help him go there. Their destinies (his, Dinah's and all the Shapiros') were now tied to Benjamin's promises and determination to give Hannah her wish — to leave Russia.

Toward the end of August, a few weeks before the Jewish New Year, Rosh Hashanah, and the Day of Atonement, Yom Kippur, the most sacred day in the Jewish calendar, Uncle Ara thrust a telegram into Judah's hands:

LETTER RECEIVED STOP PREPARING STOP LETTER FOLLOWS CHANA W.

"What good is a telegram?" Benjamin exploded. "We need more than a telegram!"

"But we know they received the letter, Papa," Gissia patiently explained. "They said they were preparing and that is good news. Be calm, Papa. The letter will come soon enough."

"How can you all be so relaxed?" Cera scolded her sisters. "Don't you know, any of you, what is going on? Don't you know they are still saying 'down with the Czar'? And if we do not leave this country soon — before they pull him down, and that could be any minute — we may never be able to leave!"

"That will be a good thing if the Czar goes down," Minya replied. "We might end up with a better country, better for us as Jews, if that happens. There are a lot of young people working to bring justice to Russia."

"Enough," Hannah snapped. "I want to hear no more of this. We shall hear what we have to hear when the time comes. In the meantime, I do not see any improvements in our future if we stay. Now, we shall all remain calm — everyone!"

Rosh Hashanah came to a crowded synagogue in Krolevets in mid-September. Benjamin sat on the first floor worshipping with the men while Hannah sat in the balcony overlooking the sanctuary with the women, wondering and fearful.

Her heart was in the meager house of Uncle Simon, Simon the bagelmaker, in Abrijilki. The children had been hurriedly taken there the day before the holiday began to be safe from the newest threat to bedevil their lives.

"You will do this for me, Uncle Simon; do it for the memory of your sister, my mother — may she rest in peace — and for all the corned beef," Benjamin told him before the old bagelmaker could object. "We hear there will be trouble in Krolevets over the holidays. So you will keep the children safe and sound."

"Here? In Abrijilki? Who can be safe here, Benjamin? This is foolishness!"

"No. This is the best place. Nothing will happen in this shtetl, Uncle Simon, as long as you go on giving your bagels to

[85]

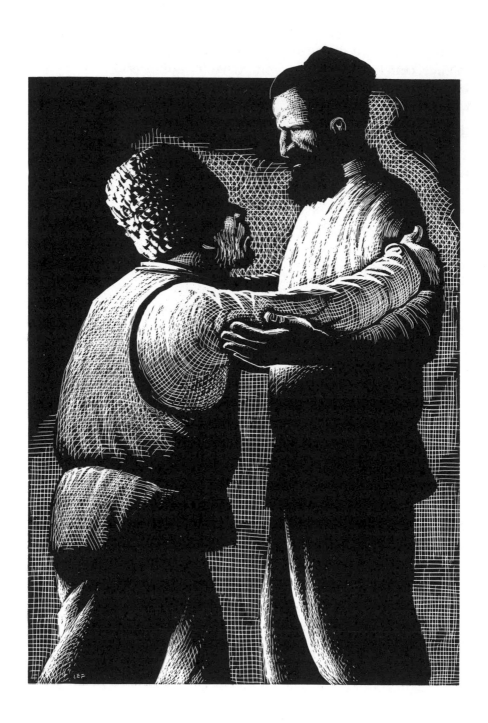

the soldiers. Besides, not even the peasants have heard of Abrijilki. So this is probably the safest place in all of Russia."

"How can you do this to me, Benjamin? This is a terrible responsibility! I am too old! All these children!"

"Don't concern yourself. You'll have plenty of help. Gissia, Minya, Shana, and Cera — look at them. Do they look like children to you? They are women. They'll help!"

"Children!" Simon insisted. "What will I feed them? Bagels? Beets? A little borscht? You have brought a basket of food. How long do you think it will last? What will I do if they get hungry and we have nothing left?"

"If they get hungry, Simon, tell them to go to sleep."

"Where? This is only one room!"

"On the floor," was Benjamin's laconic answer.

Benjamin pressed some money into his uncle's hand. "You may need this," he told him. He left his tearful children and went back home to Krolevets, mumbling that God should be good to them and watch over them.

Twice, in late September and early October, the Shapiro children were sent to Abrijilki in response to warnings of calamity and in the face of the rising tumult throughout Russia.

"Give us a voice," the people howled at the Czar. "Give us a parliament! Give us a constitution!"

The country teetered on the edge of insurrection and chaos. The Czar consulted his ministers. They advised him to grant a parliament, a Duma, and a constitution with guarantees of free speech, free press, and freedom to assemble.

"That will stop these infernal demonstrations? Yes?"

"Yes, Your Imperial Majesty."

"Good. Give them a Duma. Give them a constitution and

[87]

whatever goes with it. Free this and free that. Then, as soon as everything is back to normal and quiet, take it all back! Everything! No parliament! No constitution! I do not intend to share my authority or reign with chronic complainers!"

In October, after things had indeed calmed down with the granting of the Duma and constitution, the Czar and his ministers took it all back. They blamed Jewish agitators, spies, and revolutionaries for all the trouble. The country exploded in violence. Instead of laying this treachery where it belonged, at the feet of the Czar and his government, they dragged Jews into the streets and beat them. The Jewish Defense League of Chernigov beat off their assailants as best they could. Trouble was everywhere but in Krolevets, strangely enough. Not even Abrijilki, that speck of a shtetl no one had ever heard of, escaped. It was battered to the ground and burned by a marching, running, tumbling horde of peasants who seemed to rise out of the earth. Hundreds of them, bundled in rags from their feet to their necks, armed to the teeth with pitchforks, sticks, knives, swords, and rifles, screaming, "Hep! Hep! Hep! Zid! Zid! Zid!" swarmed through the tiny impoverished village and left nothing standing or alive in their wake. And when they finally disappeared over a hill and into the next shtetl, the only sound left was the tolling of the bells of Chernigov District.

Simon had been warned by a soldier friend that this would happen on Yom Kippur eve. Panic-stricken and near hysteria with all the Shapiro children on his hands — he never told them of the fate that awaited them all if they remained — desperate Simon sneaked into the army garrison he knew so well, left a box of bagels, and took a horse and wagon. He brought it back undetected, and everyone piled in.

"We are going for a ride," Simon announced.

"At night, Uncle Simon? Why?"

"To clear the lungs. Don't ask so many questions."

Simon whipped the horse into a frenzy and they went careening on two wheels into the night an hour before Abrijilki and its inhabitants disappeared from the face of the earth.

Somehow, Simon's sense of direction got them to a small building near a railroad track. No one had any idea where they were, least of all Simon. There was only the small building and the track. There were no signs.

"We will stay here," Simon told his shaken charges, who now knew why they had fled. "If God sees us, He will send a train. And if it stops here, you will all get on."

"But where will it take us, Uncle Simon? We have never been on a train at night, only in the daytime going to Konotop or Bakhmach."

"Who knows? What difference does it make? There is always a first time. You will be safer on a train going somewhere — anywhere. Night or day, it's the same train. Here, Gissia, before I forget; here is the money your papa gave me. Use it for train tickets."

"Aren't you coming with us, Uncle Simon?"

"No," said the old bagelmaker. "You will be better off without me. I am too old to run anymore. But I shall stay with you until God sends the train — if God is willing, of course. Don't worry, I shall be all right. And you older ones. You make sure you take care of the little ones. Don't leave anyone behind. There are a lot of you, you know."

God was willing. A train crept to a halt at the little building around daybreak. A man got off. Eleven people got on. There was no one else on the train except a burly conductor fast asleep and snoring loudly at the rear of the car the children entered. The train moved on as Uncle Simon waved and passed out of their lives, forever.

"Shhh," Gissia cautioned everyone as she propped sleeping baby Dvera against Shana. "Don't wake her up. If she stays asleep we shall be better off."

"Where are we, Gissia?" Rivka and Mera wanted to know. They were near tears but too frightened to cry. "We're hungry."

"Shhh. I don't know where we are. Soon it will be lighter and then maybe we will be able to tell. Go to sleep."

The train jerked along at half speed. It did not seem to be in a hurry. A hot cast-iron stove in the center of the car steamed the windows against the cool early-morning light. The conductor slept on. Rivka, Mera, and Feiga fell asleep, exhausted. Rochlia and Rachmael took turns watching them as everyone else — Gissia, Minya, Shana, Cera, and Ita — kept wiping the steam from the windows to see if they could spot a familiar sight, a landmark, something. There was nothing but a near-treeless landscape on one side of the tracks and a forest on the other. The forest seemed familiar. The look of the place had a special feeling.

"The train is slowing down."

"It is going to stop."

"Here! You kids!" The conductor was awake now. "Where did you come from?"

"The little station b–b–back there," Gissia explained, beginning to stammer and shake with terror.

"What little station?"

"The little house with the t–t–tools in it."

[90]

"That was no station. That was a maintenance shed."

"B–b–but the train s–s–stopped there to l–l–let us on."

"Sure it did. But not to let you brats on. It stops there every morning to let Georgi off."

"Georgi?"

"Yes. Georgi. The relief fireman on this train. He lives near there. What's it to you kids anyway? Where are your tickets?"

"W–w–we d–d–don't have any," Gissia chattered, convinced that none of them would live through the next five minutes.

"Where are you going?"

"K–k–krolevets?" Gissia hoped.

"Well, you'd better pay up quickly — one kopek each. That'll be — let's see — one, two, three — eleven kopeks altogether. We stop in Krolevets in exactly two minutes," said the conductor as he checked his watch.

"Look!" Ita screamed. "Krolevets! It's Krolevets. We're home!"

"And there's Papa! and Suchenko! and Uncle Tevya!" Shana pointed out as she kept hiking the sleeping Dvera in her arms.

"Another miracle," Cera exclaimed hysterically.

They jammed their faces against the cool, watery windows to see the miracle as the train screeched and hissed to a halt. Gissia pressed some coins into the conductor's meaty hands and they scrambled off the train. Gissia counted each of them including herself as they all detrained.

"Papa! Papa!"

Benjamin Shapiro, in animated conversation, his back to the departing train, whirled around at the rush of familiar voices. Dumbfounded, he was quickly engulfed by a leaping, jumping crowd of his own children who nearly knocked him over with their joyful enthusiasm.

[92]

"Where did you come from?" Benjamin was stunned.

"What were you doing on that train? Uncle Simon? Where is Uncle Simon?"

By the time everyone had caught their breaths, Gissia had told her father, her uncle, and Gregor Suchenko about their flight from Abrijilki. The pain and relief on Benjamin's face was evident. He and Tevya had come to see Suchenko before going to the synagogue on Yom Kippur morning. They had heard that a number of small villages were destroyed during the night but had no idea whether or not Abrijilki was one of them. They thought perhaps Suchenko might have some information. He did not.

All Benjamin knew was that he had deposited his children at a "safe" shtetl which could have lost its secure status. It had. But the children were safe and back where they belonged. For the moment, Benjamin could not absorb the details. He just said, "God is being good to us." Now he could go to the synagogue on this holiest of days and repent — for what he did not know — and beg forgiveness — for what he could not even guess. "For being alive and a Jew?" he asked himself.

His real mission today was to thank God for delivering his children and to plead with Him to end the madness.

"If You could only do this, God, we might not have to leave. We might be able to live happily in Russia. I am a Russian, am I not?" he insisted. "Sure I am a Jew, but still a Russian. Is this not my land, the land of my father, the land of his father, and of his father before him?"

But God's answer came in a hail of rocks thrown through the new windows of the restored synagogue. Whatever hope there may have been was shattered like the glass. Now Benjamin knew that a different destiny awaited them all somewhere far away, however many Shapiro generations he counted in Krolevets.

Three days later the letter came. "And just in time," Hannah thought and said as much to Benjamin.

Dear Hannah and Benjamin:
We are making arrangements for Gissia, Shana, Cera, and Ita as fast as we can. It is not as simple as we thought. This is what we have done. We have reserved with the Holland–American Steamship Company in New York four single female sea passages – one-way steerage from Rotterdam (Holland) to New York, departing in early February 1906. The shipping people advised us that they cannot guarantee unreserved passages before that date. So we gave them $30 deposit with $90 more due when they give us the departure time and ship and whatever else is needed. We will pay everything here. The girls will have to pay nothing there in Rotterdam. They will have to come to Rotterdam by train (they say that is the best way) and be in that city at least two days before sailing. Their tickets will be waiting for them in the offices of the Holland–American Line. They are to go directly to the office and present their passports and the other documents required by the Czar. They will need warm clothing and about an extra $35 (70 rubles) if you can manage it. The ocean voyage will be about eighteen days and they will have to have money to eat and to stay in a hotel before departure time. You will hear from us by telegram as to the exact details. We have already satisfied the American officials here that we will guarantee a place for our nieces. God bless you and keep you. David says hello.

Chana

⚈ SEVEN ⚈

"Is everyone here?" Hannah asked as she surveyed her brood crowding around the brass menorah. Eight candles were in place on the nine-branch candlestick used to commemorate Hannukah. "Gissia? Minya? Shana? Cera? Cera??"

"Cera!" Benjamin called out. "Didn't you hear your mother? What are you doing at the window? Come away from there!"

"There is someone or something out there, Papa. The dogs are growling."

Everyone in the large kitchen froze. Benjamin, who had been holding Dvera, calmly gave her to Hannah. Slowly, deliberately, he walked over to Cera, put his arm around her, cocked his head and listened. The older children sidled over to the younger children. Deaf-mute Feiga was too young and handicapped to understand the moment. Minya picked her up and rocked her gently. Shana and Gissia held hands with Mera and Rivka, both of whom were puzzled by the sudden change of tone, although they knew that things like this had happened before. Ita and Rochlia moved closer to their mother. Rachmael elected to stand next to his father and Cera at the window.

Outside, beyond the fence, several men stood ankle-deep in the soft snow watching the wood-and-stucco house on the knoll. Two more shadowy figures joined them as the sun slid down behind the dry, wintry trees. A new snow began to fall. By morning, the snow would be knee-high.

Somewhere in the bluish, snowy stillness of this Thursday evening (the beginning of the seventh day of Hannukah, the eight-day Jewish Festival of Lights), the happy tinkling of sleigh bells floated on the crisp, distant air. There was laughter.

[95]

"Alexei! Please!" a ghostly, girlish voice giggled and pleaded as it trailed off into the twilight. A couple of dogs barked. And then nothing. Quiet.

"Well, Serge," exclaimed Mayor Grozni with a sweep of his arm, "this is what you wanted to see, the house of the Jew Shapiro. There it is. Is that not correct, Nikolai?" Grozni asked his police chief, Tartazov. "And also, for your information, that house down there by the river bank belongs to Leonid Cherniskov, the shoemaker. He is not a Jew. Neither is his wife. They have no children."

"Now what?" Tartazov wanted to know. "Why are we here in the middle of a blizzard? Can't your men here burn down Shapiro's house some other time? Shapiro is going nowhere. He will be there tomorrow, and the next day, and the next."

"Don't be too sure," replied the man called Serge.

"We have sent some patriots here from time to time to show your Jews a thing or two, and they are still here!"

"Perhaps Tartazov is right, Serge. Let us return to the inn. It is warmer there. We'll make plans. It is beginning to snow too hard. We'll burn Shapiro when the snow stops."

"So," Serge said, "that is the house of the Jew Shapiro, provisioner to the Czar."

"We already told you that, Serge, if you please."

"Please, Boris Grozni. I must make my report. I am sorry if I was delayed and have only just arrived with my assistants. But, you see, I had to make sure that the records I received from the registrar of Chernigov were of the right Shapiro. This Jew has friends in the army. We must be careful. That is why it is better to make my inspection at dusk. Why should we reveal ourselves when we do not have to — yet."

"Can we go now, Serge?" Mayor Grozni whined, not want-

[97]

ing to offend the provincial official, his superior, whose job it was to organize attacks on Jews.

"Did you know, Boris, that the Chernigov Jews have formed an armed league for self-defense?" Serge went on, paying not the slightest attention to what anyone else was saying. "Since October, we have had our hands full. They fight! Did you ever hear of such a thing? Jews fighting? Preposterous! But that is the way it is. Absolute foolishness. It goes very hard with them. We have had to become more severe. A group of particularly vicious yeshiva boys — twenty or thirty of them — religious school boys, mind you, attacked a soldier home on leave to see his dying mother. They knocked him down, dragged him into an alley, and like the mad dogs that they are, they were about to drink his blood!"

Grozni and Tartazov looked at each other with a mixture of resignation and disbelief. They had heard such tales time and again. They rarely believed any of them.

"But the police caught the hooligans just in time. Several of them got away. But we know who they are. The soldier was dead, of course. The mad dogs were brought before the magistrate within minutes. We hanged the three ringleaders right then and there. The others are on their way to Siberia. We'll catch the rest sooner or later. Be on your guard, Boris. There must be no such self-defense league in Krolevets! Be on your guard!"

"Not in Krolevets!" both the mayor and police chief exclaimed.

"Good!" said Serge. "We'll go back to the inn now and make a few plans for the Jew Shapiro and maybe some of his friends."

Inside the house on the knoll, Benjamin Shapiro finally

[98]

spoke. "There are no bells. We have received no warnings from anyone. I cannot hear anything. I cannot see anything through the fence. The dogs are absolutely quiet. I do not think we need to worry. Besides, who would be out on a night like this? Let us get on with Hannukah. The sun is already down and on the other side of the world. Rachmael, it is your turn. Remember now, before you set fire to the menorah, you must tell us a little about Hannukah."

No one relaxed as Rachmael nervously raced through all that he knew about the holiday in one breath.

"It's about the Maccabees and the Temple," Rachmael offered.

"That's not bad," Benjamin told his son with humorous sarcasm in an attempt to lighten the atmosphere and make the fear disappear. "Perhaps by the time of your Bar Mitzvah you will know the whole story."

"But that is five years away," Hannah protested, coming to the defense of her son.

"I know," Benjamin replied, feigning weariness, "that gives Rachmael plenty of time to find out the details. In the meantime," Benjamin added as Hannah lit the central candle, "it is time to light seven more candles."

Rachmael took the candle his mother had lit for him and, as his older sisters and mother recited the special prayer, he touched its flame, one by one, to the seven candles. The eighth and final candle would be lit tomorrow night.

Hannah and Benjamin looked at each other across the glowing menorah and tried to understand the future.

❧❧ 1906 ❦❦

⌗ ONE ⌗

The telegram lay face up on the kitchen table. Benjamin, Hannah, and the older children stared at it. No one wanted to pick it up or touch it after Benjamin had brought it home from Suchenko's telegraph office. It was as if it carried a contagious disease. Chana and Samuel Weinstein had sent the telltale news to Krolevets instead of to Konotop as they had been instructed to do.

"The cat is out of the bag now," Benjamin declared. "Suchenko knows. Soon everyone will know, including Tartazov. I suppose they all have to know sooner or later, and the time is now."

Benjamin read the telegram aloud. It was the third or fourth time he had done so. There was no turning back, and Benjamin could hardly believe it.

RECEIVED KROLEVETS CHERNIGOV OBLAST RUSSIA 14 JANUARY 1906
BENJAMIN SHAPIRO
SEND THREE STOP SS NOTTERDAM DEPARTS ROTTERDAM NETHERLANDS
18 FEBRUARY STOP 5 FEBRUARY RUSSIAN TIME STOP CONTACT
HIAS* ARRIVAL ROTTERDAM STOP
CHANA W.

The family in New York had purchased only three one-way

*Hebrew Immigration Aid Society

[104]

passages from Rotterdam to New York. Ninety dollars was all they could afford.

Benjamin decided that Cera would stay home. "We are still in business. Where in Krolevets do you think I can find a bookkeeper who can count? Gissia, Shana, and Ita will prepare the way."

Cera protested. An adventure by rail across all of Europe and by ship across the Atlantic Ocean to America without Mama or Papa or the rest of the brood was an exciting, intriguing prospect. "I am more necessary than Ita. I am a bookkeeper. I am older. I can find work." But her protests fell on deaf ears. Benjamin had made up his mind that if something should go wrong, it was more important that Cera be in Krolevets near him than in New York. Benjamin had her name scratched from the recently acquired passport.

"Don't worry," he told everyone, "in six months time, maybe seven — no more, perhaps less — we shall all be together again in America."

"But why can't we all go now — together?" young Rivka demanded.

"No more silly questions," snapped Hannah near tears, as the coming separation loomed as a vivid reality.

Hannah could hardly explain her frustration at their inability to emigrate as a whole family at once. The answer was simple enough: there was a lack of ready cash on both sides of the ocean — money needed to take a family of thirteen from one side of the world to the other safely.

"I shall not run from here," Benjamin repeated over and over again. "I shall not be anyone's beggar! And neither shall my wife and my children! We shall leave this place as we have

[105]

lived here, with respect! And we shall arrive there and live there (he could not bring himself to say 'America') as we have here in Krolevets.''

Benjamin had extended too much credit at the delicatessen. A number of old customers were unable to pay. Benjamin refused to press them. It would not have helped anyway. None of them had any money. Some customers had gone to America and elsewhere, leaving large unpaid bills. Chief of Police Tartazov was extorting money regularly from Benjamin in return for what was fast promising to become a dubious guarantee of protection from anti-Jewish violence. Moreover, the army was holding up payments for provisions delivered. The Ninth Army Corps Quartermaster had not paid Benjamin and others one kopek since the naval mutiny in Odessa a year ago, pending the outcome of an investigation that had never begun.

The Czar himself had ordered Eighth Army Headquarters in Odessa to look into the mutiny. A court of inquiry was established. It never convened. The navy refused to appear, objecting vehemently to an army court investigating naval matters. The army, embarrassed by the Czar's peculiar, troublemaking order and worried over its own failures in the Far East (it certainly did not want the navy looking into army affairs), kept arguing over a convenient date for the inquiry. The bungling stalemate created by the Czar's administrative clumsiness, if not complete stupidity, affected all those doing legitimate business with a military whose mutinies, ineffectiveness, and disasters were rooted in an incapable and indifferent imperial government.

''Pending completion of His Majesty Czar Nicholas II's Court of Military Inquiry regarding recent complaints occurring in

[106]

naval units assigned to the station Odessa, all monies due and payable to citizen vendors licensed in the Eighth, Ninth, and Twenty-first Army Corps sectors are hereby impounded until further notice."

Benjamin had no idea when, if ever, he or anyone else would be paid by the army. He and Hannah decided that since they had already set aside some money to send four children to America — a voyage that would now involve three children — they would go along as planned, trusting that the army would honor its payments within the year.

"If they do not meet their obligation to us, Hannah, neither Hilya nor Tevya will have the cash to help us. Then what?"

"Don't think about it, Benjamin. Just get the necessary papers and train tickets. We shall send the girls regardless. And we shall follow them, somehow."

The documents were secured: passport and visas in Chernigov; residency certificate and travel permits in Krolevets; and trans-European train tickets, second-class coach reserved, in Bakhmach. Officially, the combined transaction came to ninety-seven rubles and five kopeks. Unofficially, it was a few rubles more. Benjamin was forced to pay various clerks, including the chief registrar of Chernigov, for "personal services" beyond the stated rates of the papers. Police Chief Tartazov, now fully aware of the Shapiro plans since it was his office that had to issue the proof of residency and travel permit papers, demanded his share for "personal services," in addition to what Benjamin was already paying him for "protective services."

"I have been a friend to you, Shapiro. I have seen to it that you, your family, and your property have received preferential treatment. There have been numerous threats made against

[107]

you and your property by unsavory characters. But I have stood in the path of these hooligans. Now, would you want any unforeseen regulations to arise to prevent your beautiful daughters from leaving our beautiful country?"

"No," replied Benjamin as he paid Tartazov directly.

"I'd like to kill him," Hilya growled.

If Hilya Shapiro had a scheme for disposing of the despised Tartazov, he had little time to think it through. Nikolai Tartazov died of a heart attack at his desk two days before Gissia, Shana, and Ita were to depart for the United States.

Gregor Suchenko, breathless, happily relieved of his complicity with the nasty Tartazov, if not his guilt, delivered the news to Benjamin himself.

"Everything is going to go well with you now, my friend. This is a true sign."

"If you say so, Suchenko. But tell me, do you think the next chief of police will be any different?"

❧ TWO ❧

The leaden gloom hung as heavily over the Shapiro household on the final day of January 1906 as it did over the rest of the northern Ukraine. Snow had fallen on and off since the year began. It had snowed again during the night, leaving a white dust to freshen the colorless scene. Daylight seemed only a few tones lighter than night. There was no sun. No moon. There were only the dreary contrasts of gray and the endless drifts of snow that covered the bleak, black earth.

Judah had taken the three large-belted canvas bags and two smaller ones over to the station on a sleigh. He registered the luggage with Stationmaster Suchenko through to Bakhmach. There were no other station workers as in the larger towns and cities.

"The girls will have to find a regular *nosilshtchik* (porter) after this," Suchenko told Judah, handing him the receipts and claim checks for the luggage. "And mind now, I shall ring the first bell fifteen minutes before departure time; the second bell five minutes before departure time; and if they hear the third bell, it will have been too late — they will have missed the train. Tell them to be here at half-past four sharp. That will be time enough to give them seat numbers. Seats are not reserved for them between Krolevets and Bakhmach, only after."

Judah returned to the quiet house more depressed than he cared to admit. He wandered around the yard aimlessly, looked in on the livestock, and finally trudged through knee-high snow toward the kitchen with a few pieces of peat for the stove. His and Dinah's own pending emigration to Palestine was still too distant to be real. The Shapiros' flight was the more imminent and dramatic change in his life. He would miss them.

The scene in the kitchen was not much different from what Judah was feeling. Benjamin was hunched over a steamy glass of tea, staring at nothing. Hannah tried to busy herself by arranging and rearranging some shelf crockery that had never been arranged before. Dinah was tearfully stirring a pot of scalding goat's milk that Benjamin had refused to drink, although the dull ache in his stomach had returned. Dvera was playing with a small rag doll at Dinah's feet. Leonid Cherniskov, their shoemaker neighbor, and his wife had come to say good-bye. They had brought a gift, three gifts — a pair of shoes for each of the girls — and sniffled their way out of the house. Tevya sat like a stone, holding his baby daughter. His wife was home, bedridden, expecting another child. Hilya had been there earlier but left, promising to be at the station. The younger children, from six-year-old Mera up, were huddled around the pale travelers, listening to Minya outline once again the itinerary.

"Don't forget," she instructed them, "Uncle Ara will be at the Konotop Station. When you get to Bakhmach, Aunt Etarivka and Uncle Louis will meet you and put you on the proper train. It is all arranged. But if for some reason you miss them, you are to take the 7 p.m. Romny–Libau Express north-bound to Vilna in Lithuania. Don't worry; everything is written down for you on this paper. You should be in Vilna by noon tomorrow; however, it is possible that the train will be late."

Minya went on to tell them once again how they would get to Vilna where they would transfer to a westbound Trans-European Express. That train would take them to Berlin, Germany, and they would leave Russia forever at a place called Verzhbolovo — a border crossing into Germany also known as Wirballen. In Berlin they would change again to another train, also westbound, which would take them straight through to Rotterdam.

"Remember now," Minya cautioned, "you are to go directly to the offices of the Hebrew Immigration Aid Society in the Rotterdam station no matter what time it is. Somebody will be there to direct you to the office of the Holland–American Line where you will show them your papers and they will give you your tickets and direct you further. Remember, too, that the HIAS person will see you to a hotel."

"Papa?" Gissia asked quietly. "Promise us we will see you and Mama and everyone else soon, this year. Please, Papa, promise." Gissia fought back her tears.

"Promise them, Benjamin! Promise all of us, Benjamin! Or else this is no good. In another hour they will be gone. And I will not live out the rest of my life with three children in America and the rest of us here. Promise us, Benjamin!"

Benjamin looked up slowly. "I said it before and I say it again: in six months' time the rest of us will be in America. There must be no more tears, only courage. I promise," he repeated softly, wondering if God would let him keep his promise. With that he handed Gissia seventy rubles to be distributed among the three of them for the trip.

◙ THREE ◙

A pack of children silently ran alongside the two sleighs full of Shapiros, escorting the horse-drawn vehicles to the station door. The pleasant music of the tinkling sleigh bells was quickly drowned out by a noisy dissonant wail that rose from the throats of several hundred people who greeted their arrival. The jostling crowd immediately jammed the sleighs, preventing anyone from dismounting.

A hundred hands holding letters, parcels, or nothing at all

were thrust at the passengers. "I have a married daughter in Brooklyn," shouted a bony old man as he shoved an envelope into the first sleigh. "Please give her this." Gissia took the envelope as the old man fell and crawled beneath the sleigh to keep from being trampled by others with urgent messages.

"I have a brother in Philadelphia. . . . Do you remember Zena? . . . My sons are in Brooklyn. . . . Can you give this to my sister in Chicago? . . . Grandchildren in Baltimore . . . Hester Street . . . Rivington . . . Delancey . . . Please? . . . Can you? . . . Will you? . . . Look up Aaron Ber. . . . Say hello to Chai. . . . Good-bye, Gissia. . . . Farewell, Shana. . . . Good luck, Ita. . . ."

Some of the crowd tried to climb into the sleighs but were pushed off by Benjamin, Tevya, and feisty Cera. Hilya, who had been waiting at the station, could not readily get through the crowd to help at the sleighs. Somehow, he and Suchenko, with the help of one or two cooperative youths, cleared a path for the travelers and got them off the sleighs and into the small overheated stationhouse. Suchenko quickly locked the doors as the crowd pressed the building on all sides and spilled over onto the tracks.

There was no mistaking the three slightly disheveled young travelers on their way to America. Gissia, Shana, and Ita wore identical new blue ensembles crafted especially for the trip by Shana's incomparable hands. The girls were not only a burst of color in a dreary tapestry of gray, they were a vision of stylishness in a place not often given over to fashion. Shana and the girls had found magazine pictures of the latest Paris styles. Shana did the rest, duplicating the pictorial images out of material Benjamin had bought many months ago in Chernigov and which Hannah had tucked away for some special occasion.

[113]

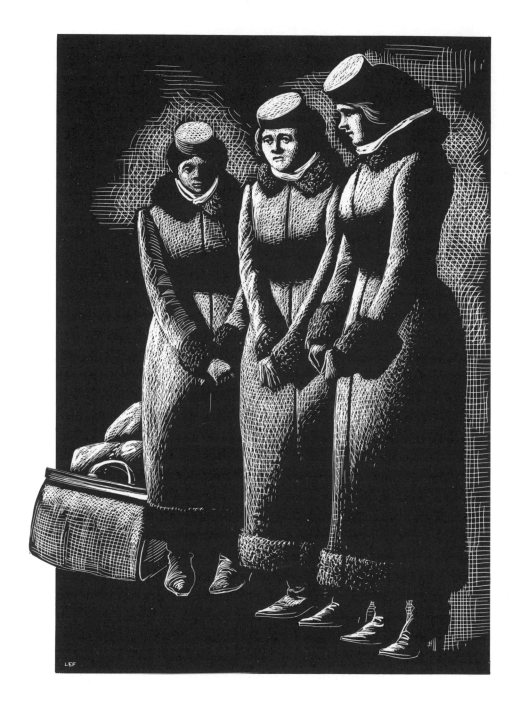

Small, round pillbox hats were rakishly tilted above their eyes. Their form-fitting, ankle-length cloth coats were trimmed with black lamb's wool on the collar, cuffs, and hem. They wore calf-length black leather boots made by Leonid Cherniskov and bright white, soft woolen mufflers, gifts from Rabbi Sarchefsky and family. Their black leather gloves were from Hilya and Tevya. Hannah insisted they carry the muffs that matched their coat trim but the girls packed them away instead. They decided that it would be difficult enough to manage baggage, documents, money, a basket of food, and as it turned out, dozens of letters for delivery in America — letters thrust at them moments ago.

The din inside the station rose and fell as the nervous entourage waited for the train. Gissia, Shana, and Ita stood quietly to one side of their family, unable to escape the sudden tearful embrace of this one or that.

"One more squeeze," Ita joked, trying to make light of the drama, "and we'll be dead before we see the train."

"If it does not come in five minutes," Shana added, "I shall faint."

"And I shall not go at all," Gissia whispered to Cera.

"Good! You stay. I'll go. I can be ready in three minutes," Cera whispered back, still nettled over her own cancellation from the adventure.

"Quiet! Everyone!" Suchenko bawled. "It is coming! The train is coming!" And he rushed outside to ring the bell to clear the tracks. He had forgotten the fifteen minute three-bell schedule of the Russian railroad system.

The human noise snapped off. The assemblage listened. They heard a distant whistle over Suchenko's clanging bell.

[115]

Another, closer. The crowd on the tracks scattered to the northbound side. A collective moan arose from the family in the waiting room. Hannah tried to smother her daughters all at once, in one last embrace. Benjamin gently, but firmly, separated them. Gissia, Shana, and Ita, speechless and streaming tears, headed out the wrong door (the station entrance, now unlocked) instead of toward the platform door opposite. Hilya turned them in the right direction as Tevya, Judah, and Suchenko wrestled with the baggage.

Another whistle. The braking engine hissed and screeched past the station, dragging the rest of the train a quarter of a mile down the track. Already a half hour late, the train took another five minutes backing into the station. Suchenko rattled his bell frantically and urged the young ladies to climb aboard. He had already collected their tickets, given them their seat assignments, and kissed them good-bye and safe journey from "an old friend of your father's" who "remembered when you were born." Benjamin boarded the train with his daughters while Hilya and Tevya made sure the baggage was properly stowed and ticketed. The three young women hung on to their father with desperation as Suchenko rang the bell.

"Be good, my children. Be safe. God watch over you. Remember, six months." Benjamin kissed his daughters, disengaged himself with some effort, and leaped from the rolling train as Suchenko rattled the bell in farewell.

✒ FOUR ✒

Benjamin and Hannah were about to enter the synagogue Friday night at sundown several days following their daughters' departure when a runner from Suchenko's telegraph office brought them the message:

ARRIVED SAFELY ROTTERDAM STOP ALL IS WELL
GISSIA

And on another Friday night three weeks later a telegram was delivered to Hannah and Benjamin as they left the synagogue at the conclusion of the evening service:

ARRIVED SAFELY AMERICA STOP ALL IS WELL
GISSIA, SHANA, ITA

Benjamin and Hannah read the dramatic message and wept together at the synagogue door.

◙ FIVE ◙

Now it was August 31 in Krolevets. A mountain of baggage had been delivered by Judah to Suchenko at the station early in the morning. Benjamin watched the wagon leave the yard and wandered over to the cemetery to say good-bye at the graves of his parents. Hannah watched him go and hoped her husband would not suddenly, unaccountably change his mind.

Events had moved rapidly since that Monday, June 19, when the Ninth Army Corps Quartermaster surprisingly paid his provisioners.

"Not another day, another week, another month!" Hannah insisted. "One more pogrom and we shall die here. We must be gone before the holidays, Benjamin. Before, not after!"

Two days later, Benjamin was in Chernigov applying for a passport. It would take a month to collect all of the documents. In the meanwhile, Benjamin sold the business to his brothers. Tevya bought the house and everything that went with the property.

"You are foolish, Benjamin. Things are improving in Russia. You are making a mistake. You will never be happy in America. You belong here. There is a new constitution. The Czar must now listen to the people. It is a new day. It is not too late," Tevya maintained.

"Don't say these things to me, Tevya," said Benjamin, as he signed the legal papers turning business and property over to his brothers at one minute past midnight, September 1. "We are going to take the fastest and most direct way out of here. Overnight by train to Libau. That train is at last going to do a

[118]

good service! Libau is half the distance the girls traveled to Rotterdam, and three weeks later — poof! America! From what I hear they have a constitution too. The same for everybody — Jew, Gentile, atheist, pagan — the same for everybody. Not like here, a constitution for them and rocks for Jews!"

"It's finished, Mama. It's ended, Papa," Benjamin told the gravestones. "We are going to America. Our grandchildren will not be Jews in Russia. They will be Jews in America. It's better that way. Not so much for me and Hannah, but for them, the unborn. We have been in this land a long time. Maybe too long, and it is time for a change. We are not the first to do this, you know. We are probably the last. Better now than never, I think. Good-bye, Mama. Good-bye, Papa."

The sorrow of parting from the dead as well as the living drifted out of a mystically rooted sense of things past and long forgotten but always present in the unidentifiable stream of Jewish consciousness. It floated in and out like so many sighing ghosts to remind the Jew of his eternal connections. For Benjamin Shapiro, the oldest son of an oldest son, to give up the black earth of the Russian Ukraine was a jolting act of removal from a continent upon which he and his ancestors had grimly, restlessly lived for eight centuries. It mattered little that Tevya, Hilya, his sister Etarivka, and other lines of Shapiros would remain on the black earth; he, Benjamin Shapiro, was the head of the family. It was his going that broke the continuity, the bond with the past.

Benjamin walked away from the cemetery. The morning dampness was fast evaporating as a warm sun heated up the day and his back. The dull, faint ache in his stomach persisted. His physician brother-in-law, Herschel Borodin, once recommended a long sea voyage to help relax his stomach in the event the goat's milk did not work.

"I don't need the goat anymore," Benjamin mused as he roamed through the pear orchard that would soon belong to Tevya and entered a thick pine grove. "Herschel said a sea voyage. A sea voyage it will be."

He stopped for a moment and recalled against his will the terrible events of the recent spring which he did not want to remember; it was not many weeks after Gissia, Shana, and Ita had landed in America, during Holy Week and Passover, that they were all driven from the house and had to hide in this very grove.

"And we are still alive," Benjamin muttered. "A miracle!"

He kicked at the needle-covered dirt where they had buried a few cherished possessions: the menorah, a brass mortar and pestle that had belonged to Benjamin's mother, a few photographs taken by Berkhan and Morozovski, Hannah's heirloom gold chain and watch, and the silver dinner service for twelve that had been part of her dowry, a gift of her long-gone aunt and uncle. All these things and more were carefully packed away and entrusted to Gregor Suchenko at the railroad station. Benjamin had no idea how they would ever get themselves and all their possessions to America. Hannah even insisted they take some table linen and bedding for the children, at least their favorite blankets.

"Foolishness!" Benjamin roared. "The ship will sink!"

"Nonsense!" Hannah cried.

Hannah won.

"And my brothers think there is a better day coming?" Benjamin continued to talk to himself in the grove. "What good is a

[120]

constitution to muzhiks who cannot read and to a Czar who does not want to read? And would they hate Jews less if they all did read? Bah! But what if Hilya and Tevya are right? What if a better day does come? What are we giving up? Is America so much better?"

Benjamin picked up a pinecone and absently turned it over in his hand. His mind was flooded with the terror and the bells of Holy Week at the end of last March.

It started traditionally enough that Palm Sunday. Feodor Korbeyev leaned on the bells and the first rocks were hurled at the house. If Leonid Cherniskov and Gregor Suchenko had not warned them, it would have been a bit more frightening. Benjamin and Rachmael had time to bury their valuables in the grove, while Hannah, Dinah, and the girls were hidden in Cherniskov's house once again. Judah tended the animals and unleashed the dogs. He, Benjamin, and Rachmael buried themselves in the damp straw as always. A gang of ten or fifteen young peasants kept up the barrage until a heavy rain drove them off.

The wet weather worsened and continued through the first two nights of Passover, Tuesday and Wednesday. The Passover Seder went on as usual. The entire family once again retold the story of their deliverance from Egyptian slavery. Once in a while, Korbeyev's mad bells could be heard between thunder claps and against the steady rain. Some peasants tried to set the synagogue on fire but it would not burn. In its moment of wet resistance, this inanimate building had become a living thing empowered by God Himself (or so it seemed), defying the grossest evils hurled against it. The synagogue, God's House, was inhabited by God Himself in that sinister moment.

[121]

On Thursday, without warning — it was Maundy Thursday, a holy day commemorating Jesus' washing of His disciples' feet — a dozen officials who said they represented the Chernigov Zemstva, the provincial assembly, demanded entrance to the house. Neither Benjamin, Judah, or Rachmael was home. They were at the delicatessen. The delegation, led by the familiar schoolteacher, Yuri Malinikov, also included the mysterious man called Serge who had filed a report on the "Jew Shapiro, provisioner to the Czar" last Hannukah; they demanded to see the "illegal school."

"We have no illegal school," Hannah protested.

"We know otherwise," Malinikov shouted, looking straight at Minya. He pushed Hannah and Dinah aside and marched into the house followed by his official party. The two dogs went wild on their leashes. If they had been free they would have killed Malinikov and anyone else who remained on the property who did not belong there. No one made an attempt to unleash the dogs. No one would dare. Malinikov found what he was looking for at the back of the house: a room full of tables, chairs, books — Russian books, not Hebrew books, religious or otherwise — slates, and chalk. He and his men smashed everything in sight including the windows as the man named Serge smoked a cigarette and watched. They dragged all the materials outside, heaving some of them through the broken windows, collected everything in a pile, and set the mass on fire.

"You are respected citizens of Krolevets. Consider yourselves lucky not to be under arrest. The next time you will not be so lucky. Remember, you are Jews. You must obey the law like everyone else."

"But how can our children learn to be good citizens if you do not permit all of them to study in your schools — in the regular Russian schools? If you say we are citizens, how can there be one law for you and another law for us?"

"That is not my problem," Malinikov retorted. "Take it up with the Czar."

When Benjamin, Rachmael, and Judah returned home, having heard what had happened, Benjamin's first inclination was to confront Malinikov. But that would have been useless and foolhardy. Instead, Benjamin told Minya to continue the school without tables and chairs, chalk and slate, and to use a bedroom.

"Sit on the floor. Write your numbers in the dust. I shall find you a book somewhere."

Good Friday came and went with no incident anywhere. Feodor Korbeyev, on the other hand, kept up his war of nerves. He and a friend relieved each other throughout the day and provided the town and its environs with a relentless peal of bells. The black-draped Church of Our Saviour was preparing itself for Easter.

Just before Saturday midnight on Easter eve, a great procession of priests and people carrying banners and pictures of their patron saints marched around the outside of the church. At the stroke of midnight, Korbeyev sent a peal of bells rolling across the countryside as the procession entered the church. Not a Jew in Krolevets was asleep — nor were there any Jews asleep in all of Russia. For centuries the Jews of Eastern Europe had been particularly sensitive to the officially sanctioned public expression of the Resurrection of Jesus Christ — not without reason and fear. Too many atrocious, deadly pogroms began

[123]

and ended on Easter Sunday. That they were planned and carried out on Easter Sundays was in itself a sinful act against mankind — a sin for which Christ Himself suffered on the Cross.

Feodor Korbeyev pulled at his bellrope. The priests intoned, "Christ is risen." The worshippers responded, "He is risen indeed," and congratulated themselves on the event with strenuous embraces and kisses. All the while, a couple of dozen ragtag peasant youths had crossed the Seim River and were crawling up the bushy slope toward the house of Benjamin Shapiro, Jew. With blood-curdling shrieks, they scampered up and over the slope and made for the house. The terrible cries reached the alert Shapiros in time for them to flee from the back of the property into the dark grove.

Winded, but in control, Hannah and Benjamin began a head count. "Dinah, Rochlia, Minya, Rivka, Cera, Judah, Feiga, Mera, Rachmael, Dvera. . . . Dvera? . . . Who's got Dvera? . . . Dvera! My God, we forgot Dvera!"

Benjamin rocketed out of the grove and raced back to the house unmindful of his own safety. Cera was at his heels, falling and tripping over her long skirt.

"Go back, Cera! Go back!"

Cera kept on coming. The woodshed began to burn. Benjamin turned a corner. He could see a group of marauders inside the house smashing windows, furniture, crockery. He was nearly stampeded by his own horses as they ran for freedom, riderless. Two of the peasants were trying to get at the dogs still chained to the gateposts. Judah had not had time to let them go. The peasants finally gave up and chased the horses into the night. Benjamin saw another fire out of the corner of

his eye. It was some distance away. He wondered if it was the rabbi's house. Suddenly he became aware of the bells and just as suddenly his eyes fell on Dvera sitting against the fence picking at a stone not three feet from where Fritzie, the older of the two Dobermans, had fended off the peasants. Benjamin did not wait to figure out how Dvera got there. He scooped her up and raced back to the grove, undetected.

Cera had lost her father when he had turned the corner but stumbled into Cherniskov, the shoemaker, shoveling dirt at the fire. Cera tore at the earth with her bare hands and flung a few fistsful at the flames. She gave up and returned to the grove, leaving old Cherniskov frantically heaving dirt at the flames. The woodshed burned to the ground. Luckily, nothing else did. The damage was not as severe as it could have been. Inexplicably, Suchenko and a policeman showed up several days later with three of the four horses that had galloped off. Benjamin asked for no explanation. None was forthcoming. The raid left a fear that would haunt the family.

Benjamin tried to fight off the remaining recollections of that night as he stood in the grove. Try as he might, Korbeyev's bells, the fire, and the rescue of Dvera popped in and out of his head.

Finally, he left the grove. The haunting memory, fresh and vivid, subsided. There was much to be done before the 5 p.m. train and the beginning of their voyage to a new life.

"A miracle," he repeated. "A miracle."

◪ SIX ◪

Stationmaster Suchenko stood at the edge of the platform, his feet planted wide apart, his hands loosely clasped behind his back. Roasting in his heavy new uniform of head guard, he awaited the expected crush of people who would invade the Krolevets railroad station to say *"Do svidán'ya* — farewell" to the America-bound Shapiros. Suchenko had had himself appointed head guard with two subordinate guards to handle the crowd. He remembered his lonely, near-ineffectual authority during the noisy departure of Gissia, Shana, and Ita Shapiro last January 31, seven months ago this very day.

Suchenko, perspiring and uncomfortable, motioned to his two guards that the Shapiros were coming down the dusty road. The distant train signaled its own approach with a long blast of its whistle. Unaccountably, it was nearly on time. A crowd had gathered at the station to see the Shapiros off, but not in the numbers that Suchenko had expected. Fifty or sixty people — many fewer than had seen the girls leave — had collected at the station entrance. There, silently, without expression, they watched the two wagons materialize out of the dust. Hilya drove one wagon, Tevya the other. Judah Labe was already on the station platform checking over the mountain of baggage.

Vacancy and despair flickered in the eyes of the onlookers, old and young, men, women, a few friends; not new friends, since there was no such thing as new friends in Krolevets. These were people of a lifetime and before. One old man had worked for Benjamin's father before Benjamin was born. Now they had come to witness their own separation — the living death. Neither they nor the Shapiros, the Benjamin Shapiros, would ever lay eyes on one another again. The going of Hannah and Benjamin Shapiro and all of their children to the New World, permanently, left them all numb with uncertainty.

The old order was crumbling. They, who had survived in the worst of times and always gave of themselves, had given up. Who would help them survive now? Tevya? Perhaps. Hilya? Hardly. Rabbi Sarchefsky? He had little influence. Benjamin Shapiro had a way with majors and colonels and chiefs of police. Now their shield would be gone in the train he despised, leaving them all a bit more vulnerable and isolated than they had been before.

Those who came, came to convince themselves of the sad truth. Those who did not come — and there were many — resisted the inevitable departure.

"They think that when they wake up tomorrow, it will be as it is today and yesterday," Minya sadly observed.

"They are in for a big surprise," Cera responded.

Hannah busied herself among her children, brushing back hair, straightening a belt, a dress, a collar, a coat. The train was not coming fast enough. Two years was too long a wait. The next few minutes seemed even longer.

Benjamin walked around the crowd looking here and there, grabbing a hand, leaning into a silent embrace, all the while moving his lips and saying nothing as the train slipped into the station.

Suchenko rang the first bell and announced, "Fifteen minutes. You have fifteen minutes."

Hannah shepherded her children onto the train while Ben-

jamin made sure Judah and one of the guards got all the baggage aboard.

"Five minutes," Suchenko bellowed, ringing the second bell. "You'd better get on board, Benjamin and Hannah, or the children will be in America while you are still waiting for the next train."

Benjamin looked dazed as he wished Judah and Dinah luck in their future in Palestine. Hannah began knocking at the train window, which was stuck shut. Benjamin and Suchenko shook hands. Not a word passed between them. Finally, Suchenko clapped him on the back and spun him toward his brothers, Hilya and Tevya. A frantic embrace. The train began to move. Suchenko rang the bell for the third and last time. Benjamin hopped on board the moving train and disappeared from sight, from Krolevets, never to return.

EPILOGUE

❧❧ **1907** ❧❧

The Shapiros took a direct route to Libau, Latvia, arriving there some twenty-seven hours later. They waited in Libau for three weeks until Benjamin could secure passage for the ten of them. On Sunday, October 7, 1906 on the world calendar (September 24, 1906 on the Russian calendar), the Shapiros boarded the Russian–American Line's steamship *Korea* and sailed to America. They arrived at Ellis Island on October 26 after nineteen days at sea.

At Ellis Island, their four-year-old deaf-mute daughter, Feiga, was separated from the family as an alien undesirable. She was returned to Libau, Latvia, aboard the *Korea* and then to Krolevets in the company of Minya, who left Feiga with Tevya and his wife. Minya returned a year later to the United States and was admitted. All during 1907, the family sought Feiga's return. A petition was addressed to President Theodore Roosevelt. It went astray, unanswered. They never saw Feiga again.

Hannah, who was pregnant during the entire trip, gave birth to another daughter, Lilyan, in May 1907. Lilyan Shapiro, the last of Hannah and Benjamin's children, was the first of their line born in the United States.